MIREMBE

The healing warmth of a friend

By

Hannah Ferguson

A Lupin Publication

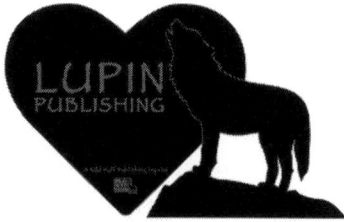

Published by Lupin Publishing in 2018
Copyright © 2018 Hannah Ferguson

Cover by Southern Stiles Design
Edited and typeset by Redwing Productions

www.wildwolfpublishing.com

For my beautiful daughter Joy Avci (1984-2014)
who taught me what mourning is

The deeper that sorrow carves into your being

The more Joy you can contain

~ *Khalil Gibran* ~

Acknowledgments

This book would not have seen the light of day if it was not for two of my dearest friends, formidable female writers themselves, Poppet and Elaina J. Davidson. It was a crazy endeavour to write a 39K book in 10 days and I will never do it again, but then to expect the hasty product to be professionally edited, formatted and published in another two weeks is downright amazing. That is what these friends stand for.

Poppet is responsible for the stunning *Mirembe* cover (and the covers of all my books) and has for the past six years been my mentor in all things writing and publishing. Elaina has over the years been my anchor, my diligent, ever-available editor and kind, inspirational friend, especially during difficult moments in my writing career.

I also want to thank my publishing house *Wild Wolf Lupin Publishing* for agreeing to bring out a book in a hurry. I feel grateful and humbled to receive this amount of support from the world of publishing.

I want to thank my colleague Wendy Keza for teaching me every day what it means to survive war and then become an empowered African woman.

Also indispensable in the birth of Mirembe has been Virginia Czarnocki, my team leader during the *Speak To Inspire* course from *London Real*. Virginia supported and cheered me on for the six weeks of the course and fully embraced my idea to bring out a book about bereavement based on my speech.

I also want to thank Susan Guner, another *London Real* team-leader, and inspirer behind the Tribe group, for the kind and persistent way in which she has guided and challenged me since I became a Tribe member in June 2018.

I thank Brian Rose for founding *London Real,* as it has changed my life beyond recognition and there is no end to the journey of growth. Inspiration, accountability, vulnerability, going where the fear is, pulling the trigger on taking action, believing in myself and my endless capacities, has become part of my daily life now. *London Real* keeps my happy, healthy and on my toes.

Finally, I want to thank my two amazing sons, Ivor and Sef. These young men keep their old mother grounded and real with their infinite love and wisdom. Or as Ivor puts it, *"Very well, Mum, these high-achievers with their constant challenges, but I worry whether you're not going too fast and getting too tired. Bereavement demands energy, you need time to give everything its proper place. So, promise me you'll take a break to recover!"*

Yes, now that Mirembe lives, I can take a little rest   …

Introduction

Mirembe approached me in October 2018 while I was stumbling through life, trying to find words to express the pain of losing my daughter. I had enrolled in the *Speak To Inspire* course from *London Real* and, during that intense process of creating a speech on bereavement, Mirembe became my haven and my point of reference. This is how strong the influence of a fictional character can be on an author. Through writing this book, however, Mirembe has now become much more than a fictional character; she has developed into an avatar for every grieving person in need of the healing warmth of a friend.

Before the *Speak to Inspire* course, I had never publicly spoken about Joy's death and what it has done to me; not since she was released from her body, destroyed by cancer, on that sunny, yet fateful day of 15 March 2014. That date will forever mark 'a before-and-after-Joy's death'.

The 'after' was sealed by budding trees along the glistening water of the River Meuse as we followed the silver-plated hearse with Joy's coffin from Erasmus MC to her final resting place in Utrecht. I was to embark on the journey of mourning my child and I had no idea how or what would be in store for me.

Mourning in the Western world is a complicated affair. For various reasons, such as our trust in longevity, a makeable life, our puritan heritage and the proliferation of individualism, we prefer to draw a veil over mourning and mourners. In particular, the death of a child or young person is not considered part of our makeup, and this results in a two-edged problem: the bereaved are clueless how to grieve, as there are no rituals to follow, and those in their orbit, already uncomfortable with the situation due to constantly inconsistent signals from their grieving member, choose to ignore or avoid the bereaved.

From the short study I conducted into bereavement in the West during my course, I found that there are few statistics or studies that give precise answers as to the complexity people face after losing a loved one and how this influences their health, career and relationships. Therefore I basically have only my own experience to relate to.

I simply shut up about the 'after' for over four years, depressed, on medication, heavily drinking and shunning contacts. Two attempts at following bereavement therapies should be called a laughing stock, had it not been so serious. The self-help group I attended just bored me as they kept us busy drawing and colouring butterflies with our child's name on it and then pinned it on a board. The advice they shared did not give me tools I could not have figured out myself. I had nowhere to turn to; no one seriously wanted to listen to what I was going through, except a very small circle of real friends, and my sons.

Speaking up during the course for the very first time about my pain was a gruelling yet cathartic experience. It helped me see how I much I had struggled – and still do – but now I feel I can possibly also help other people as much in the dark after the death of their child or a close family member. If it's part of Joy's legacy to raise the standards of dealing with grief, then she did not die in vain.

The greatest healer in my process has been Mirembe! Here is *her* story.

MIREMBE

Chapter 1

ON A BLUE MOON night in early spring one of Africa's millions of babies was born in a primitive hut on the banks of the Victoria Nile River. After a prolonged and difficult delivery, with only the assistance of a neighbour as midwife, the mother - disappointed to give birth to a daughter after the blessing of four sons - decided she would be called Kabonesa; 'trouble being born'.

The little girl's father, who had a kinder heart but never really was a match for his opinionated wife, weakly protested that his only daughter deserved a more positive name. Having enjoyed some glasses of Waragi to numb his ears to the piercing shrieks of his wife in labour, he dared to speak up, but knew it was probably useless.

Lwango never accepted argument, and now, even exhausted from childbirth and the disappointment of its sex, while hushing away Nasiche who wanted to hand her the newborn, cried angrily from her mat on the floor, "Hold your tongue, you drunken Oneka-husband. The wench is called Kabonesa, and that's the end of it!"

So that was her name, at least for the time being: trouble being born.

THE FAMILY LIVED IN a round earthen hut with a thick straw roof, the door opening veiled by a light blue cotton cloth to keep out the flies. Only two tiny windows let in enough light during the day. The simple abode possessed only one room in which all seven family members lived and slept on thin mats, scattered on a floor of hardened red mud. Most of daily life took place outside, such as cooking and washing, and the hut was generally only used to sleep. There was no other furniture, apart from a wooden cupboard that held Lwango's cooking pots and other kitchen utensils. As they owned only the clothes they wore, there was no need for other storage facilities.

Their hut stood in a wide semicircle with twenty others facing Uganda's Victoria Nile River, which provided most of their food and served as the route for transportation, not only for the hamlet's inhabitants, but also for visiting tourists.

On their cruise towards Lake Victoria, smaller vessels docked at the pontoon the villagers had created. Curious tourists wandered amongst the huts for thirty minutes, fingering the beaded jewellery the women offered, and throwing a quick glance into the primitive huts before hopping back on board to gratefully sip their martinis, a look of incredulity on their well-fed faces.

This was 1980, after all. Did people still live this way? But the villagers, with the exception of Lwango, were generally oblivious of their prehistoric circumstances. They gladly welcomed the occasional tourists for they brought in a tiny bit of extra income to spend on market day in Atura. It made them feel rich, temporarily.

Like all the other fathers of the community, Kabonesa's father was a fisherman, but what he liked most was taking long breaks from being on the river to sit smoking and talking with the other men in the shadow of the mango trees. All families had the same living standards, and all fathers did the same; nobody was interested in getting ahead in life. There was no point to it; life was what it was.

Some ten miles upstream was the nearest town, Atura, where the women went to the weekly Wednesday market, and families together on foot or by boat attended the church service in the *Pentecostal Assemblies of God* on Sundays. In Atura the villagers noticed town's people possessed cars and stone houses, but did not associate these possessions with themselves. Generally, the small river hamlet's inhabitants were content with their peaceful lives as long as their bellies were full, and the civil war did not come closer.

All but Lwango.

Lwango, now in her late thirties, was originally from Atura, where she had lived in relative wealth, born in a stone house to a father who had been a merchant before he mysteriously disappeared, and a mother who was a well-respected member of Atura's community, where she sang in the Church choir and volunteered at Atura State Hospital. Lwango had made one crucial mistake in her life; she fell in love with Oneka, who at the time looked so strong and beautiful as he carried two buckets of fresh fish into the fishmonger's shop next to her father's clothes' shop.

She married him on a whim, just to annoy her parents, which was the reason for her father's sudden disappearance and her mother being forever dissatisfied with her.

Now, fifteen years later, Lwango was extremely unhappy in her marriage, but her mother had made it clear there was no coming back to Atura, no prospect of divorce.

Grandma Sanyu, still grieving her husband's sudden vanishing, had proclaimed loud and clear from the day of her daughter's wedding, "You've made your bed, now lie in it!"

The one factor that kept bitter and jealous Lwango staying where she was were her four healthy sons. She doted on them. Fourteen, twelve, nine and seven years old, they were her absolute pride and joy.

She had wanted no more children and did all she could to keep Oneka from her mat, but the one time she gave in to him last summer had now resulted in this awful new product - a girl. If she was honest with herself, Lwango had to admit there was no reason to dislike her daughter, as the little girl was as sweet and loving and pretty as any African girl, with black furry patches on her little scalp, an as yet toothless smile and big, round eyes that followed her mother wherever she went. It was Lwango's own frustration and dissatisfaction that she directed towards the single weak female in her family.

When she was still a baby, although her mother ignored her as much as possible, Kabonesa never cried or asked for attention, so it remained relatively unnoticed that she was a neglected child. Lwango was sly enough to make sure the baby was fed and cleaned at the appropriate times; she simply never cuddled or sweet-talked her baby girl.

ONLY WHEN KABONESA WAS three years old and still did not say a word, did Lwango start to complain openly about her daughter. Every morning after the three youngest boys were at school and the eldest fishing with his father, with Kabonesa sleeping in her cot, the mother sat down with Nasiche to gossip and tea.

"Oh, Nasiche-friend, what am I do to with Kabonesa?" Lwango whined. "The girl is certainly retarded, just like her father. She will never be able to talk. She's just a nuisance."

Nasiche, as usual chewing pine tree bark because she claimed it prevented malaria and lepra, spit out a large gulp of red juice and shrugged.

"Just wait a little longer, Lwango-friend; the damsel is still very young. My Adroa didn't talk until he was five. And now I can't shut him up anymore. That mouth is either eating or talking. I only get a moment's rest when he sleeps."

Lwango wasn't that easily persuaded. "It's not just that, Nasiche-friend. She actually scares me. She just sits there all day long staring at me with those huge black marbles, as if she's looking straight into the soul God gave me."

"She has strange eyes," Nasiche agreed. "Wouldn't want my child to have such questioning eyes, but what can you do about it?"

"Well, there you go, you said it yourself!" Lwango cried out. "You wouldn't want a child like Kabonesa either. She's scary and mute. All she does is sit as a statue, staring at people. Only now and then she will play a little with the clay doll you gave her for her name day. And you know what is most outrageous? She will sing softly to herself, but never says a single word to her Mamma."

The annoyed mother sighed, readjusting her wide behind on the mat, gazing at her friend.

"Here, let me pour you another cup of mango tea," Nasiche offered comfortingly. "I agree that girls aren't much use until they have the age to help their mothers and, of course, they're useful for the dowry they bring in when they marry. But that's about all they have to offer."

Lwango secretly thought it was all very well for her friend to say that, as she had no girls of her own, but she did not want to disagree on this hot morning with lots of work awaiting her, which she dreaded. Sitting here chatting and complaining was the best moment of the day, for sure.

"Yes," she said wearily, "girls are a nuisance. You must be glad you were spared that bad omen. Boys are helpful and strong. My boys carry all the wood for the fire and I only need to snap my fingers and they will fight each other to collect the water from the river for me. Mukisa, the eldest, catches more fish than his oddball father."

It was a known and accepted fact in the hamlet that Lwango and Oneka's marriage was not a happy one, which was not any different from most couples, the only variance being that Lwango spoke about it out loud. Because of her more favoured background, she held a certain position among the villagers, who were slightly in awe of her and her sharp tongue and generally agreed with her without much contradiction.

Nasiche was not afraid of her neighbour; she was a laidback character and could not care less what anyone said or did, including Lwango. If the villagers looked into their hearts - which they did only when somebody was gravely ill or had died - they would have favoured Oneka's kinder temperament over Lwango's hoity-toity attitude, but commotions and fights were not part of their community.

In this respect Lwango was also different, what with her loud quarrels with her husband and her open dislike of her daughter.

THAT EVENING THE ARGUMENTS that fired up again was like honey being served to a bear. Oneka had had his fair share of Waragi and wanted to stop the constant nagging about his daughter.

Stroking the child's wiry, black curls, he slurred, "Ah, Lwango-wife, have some patience with her, she's only three years old. Some children don't talk until they're well over five. And her vocal cords are working perfectly because she can sing. I don't understand how you can be so hard on her; she's a lovely little girl."

Kabonesa leaned into her father, despite the fact he smelled terrible, and felt that at least one person was giving her a little warmth and love. Her brothers were under their mother's thumb, and never spoke to her or let her play with them in their games. Small as she was, the sensitive child also

29

understood that her father was only her ally when he smelled that way.

Every day she tried as hard as she could to mollify her cold-hearted mother, but never succeeded. She had tried all her sweet little tricks, such as cooing cutely, hanging on to her apron, plying her little body against her mother's soft tummy, but nothing worked. Her mother had chosen against her from the day she was born.

Lwango hated her own mother and now also hated her daughter. But she loved it when she could become querulous with her half-drunk husband.

Hands on her broad hips, and with a twist on her pronounced lips, the tall woman in her multi-coloured cotton dress snarled, "Whatever you say, Oneka-husband, you are wrong. The girl is evil. We should send her away. She just sits gazing at me all day with these big eyes, singing softly to herself, as if she wants to bewitch me. As you're not bringing in much money and I have all these mouths to feed - because eat she can - I think it's time we got rid of her. We could leave her in front of Onzia's hut and then one witch can teach the other. K already knows how to bewitch people, but I think Onzia could still teach her more of that. Now get out of my hut, both of you useless louts, and let me make dinner for those who do work."

Feeling terribly saddened and afraid she would be sent to the bent old woman who shrieked whenever someone came near her place, Kabonesa tried even harder to make her tongue talk by repeating la-la-la and bra-bra-bra. She also tried to be extra helpful to her mother, scrubbing the pots with her little hands until they shone and feeding the vegetables in the garden river water that she collected on her little legs.

APART FROM HER FATHER in his drunken state, the young child had only one other ally; her maternal grandmother Sanyu. Her grandmother lived in a proper house in the centre of Atura and was apparently well-off. Kabonesa was curious why there was no grandfather, and why nobody ever mentioned him. Also, why her grandmother lived in such different conditions was a mystery to the three year old.

She and her family visited there on the last Sunday of every month after having been to the Church service. Grandmother sat in a different part of the Church, front row, which was something Kabonesa did not understand either.

But, whenever she was in the cosy stone house on the secluded square with the coconut trees in front, the stress the sad little girl felt in her own hut subsided like smoke in the wind. They sat on real chairs in the small parlour that smelled of furniture wax instead of on the clay floor, and they drank tea from cups with roses on them.

Grandma Sanyu always smelled of roses herself. She had to like the flowers a lot because she also always wore dresses with roses on them and her little garden overflowed with rose bushes.

A slender, bare-foot black girl, not more than twelve, would come in noiselessly in her white cotton dress and serve them tea from a tray almost too big and heavy for her to carry. Grandma called her Emerald because she had light-coloured eyes, and Kabonesa was completely in awe of her. Her big eyes followed the girl around as she cautiously set down the tray and served Grandma first before the others got theirs. Emerald never looked at the visitors, but Kabonesa felt she had a connection with her and would have loved for them to play together.

Even during these visits Lwango, whose position in her mother's house was an unsure one since marrying below her standards, made an attempt at scolding her daughter.

"Sit up straight, K, and don't spoil your tea. Have you no manners at all?"

She would continue in a loud voice about what a burden her daughter was, whom she never called by her full name, and how she was too stupid to talk.

Grandma did not contradict her wilful daughter straight out these days, as the power struggle they had for years had worn out the frail-looking seventy year old with her white lace collar over her roses dress.

Once black hair was now snowy-white, cut very short, and clipped nails on long, slender fingers played nervously with her handkerchief.

Sanyu too had four sons and a late-in-life daughter, but contrary to Lwango, she had been delighted with the eleventh-hour gift from God and had spoilt her so much that the girl turned out bad and did everything to hurt her tender-hearted mother.

These days she just looked at her dissatisfied daughter and shook her head while putting an extra biscuit on Kabonesa's saucer, winking at her.

Kabonesa didn't really know what that wink meant, but she practised it herself as she understood it as a sign of goodwill.

Many times, she thought of hiding behind grandma's big mahogany bed in her upstairs bedroom so that her parents would leave her behind, but she did not dare anger her mother any further.

Little as she was, she knew that in some way things could be worse, as she had often heard the daughter of one of their neighbours scream out when her mother hit her with a stick.

At least Kabonesa's mother only used her tongue and not a stick.

Chapter 2

BECAUSE OF THEIR POVERTY there was no opportunity for Kabonesa to go to Atura's primary school as her brothers did. Her mother taught her only domestic chores, so she would be prepared to start working for one of the richer families in town when she was ten years old, and she would be married off by thirteen, just as Emerald would soon be married off.

Although tongue-tied, Kabonesa was far from stupid. In fact, she was smarter than all her brothers together, but there was no way for her to show this, as she could not express herself verbally.

She also knew from an age as early of four that she was different from the rest of her family; she could sense things they could not. She did not dream of sharing that she felt and saw things others did not, instinctively knowing she would be in even more trouble if she did.

Longing to be educated, she secretly taught herself to read and write by copying her brothers' homework in the dry mud behind their hut, going over the letters again and again until she mastered them. Reading she did even more secretly by glancing casually at their notebooks when they were out chopping wood or fishing with their father. Kabonesa had to be ever so careful; if her mother caught her doing this, she would certainly be sent to the witch Onzia. But she disobediently kept doing the homework she enjoyed, although she did not know why, considering her future was destined from birth.

At seven years old she still did not speak, but continued to sing and help her mother. She was a quiet and well-behaved girl and, apart from her mother and brothers, everyone loved her, although they looked at her a little suspiciously because of her big eyes and mute tongue.

It became harder to hide her gift. She felt it almost oozed out of her little body and everybody could see how different she was. She could not help herself; whenever someone was sick in the community and even if they died, the young girl simply sensed it and would go to the neighbours' hut and sit with the sick person until they either became better or died.

There was hardly any medical help available and only once a month a travelling doctor and two nurses visited their settlement to vaccinate babies, pull out rotten teeth and hand out malaria pills.

There was never any argument about accepting the silent girl's presence during these difficult times; on the contrary, the neighbours were grateful to her and she was often given an extra piece of bread or a small toy for her waking hours with the sick.

There was a bigger problem looming, though, and that was the power struggle between Kabonesa and her mother, a struggle the young girl did not seek but her querulous mother certainly did.

Lwango kept insisting her daughter was the younger version of the crazy Onzia, the witch, but the community more and more embraced the tender-hearted, charitable girl and stood up against the mother. This was an unprecedented situation in the close-knit hamlet, and eventually the respect for Lwango waned in favour of appreciation for her daughter.

After a long consultation between Chieftain Oidu, Nasiche, and the girl's father, Oneka, it was decided to give her the honour name of Mirembe, which meant 'peace and quiet' and seemed to suit her so much better than 'trouble being born'.

From that time onwards, only her mother continued to call her K. All others, including her father and Grandma, called her Mirembe.

ONE DAY IN EARLY August, Mirembe was eight years old, growing tall and beautiful, and feeding their three chickens with a smile of happiness on her chubby face while her mother washed her brothers' T-shirts. Both mother and daughter looked up when a black Ford slowly approached on the unpaved red sandy road that was the only land access to their settlement.

"Quickly, K, run inside and get my good apron," the mother commanded.

Knowing the girl would carry out her orders without uttering a sound, Lwango straightened her spine and, quaffing her Afro hairdo to look as dignified as she could, threw the old apron in her daughter's hand and put on the freshly starched slightly newer one, and marched towards the car.

She ordered her girl, "Get inside, K; nothing for you to see here."

This time the pliable girl obeyed her mother only partially. She did walk towards the hut, but lingered at the entrance, too curious to find out who the posh people were that had come to visit the village.

She saw a man and a woman get out of the car; they were both black, but expensively dressed, even smarter than her grandmother, but about the same age. People that also sat in the front row of the *Pentecostal Assemblies of God.*

Mirembe's sharp eyes registered that the woman had been driving, which was unheard of at the time, even by Atura standards, and this greatly puzzled the young, inexperienced girl. The lady, the only title fit for a woman of her stature, wore a cream-coloured dress with a small brown belt around her slender waist and shoes with small heels in the same colour. She was beautiful. Although completely white-haired but with very few wrinkles, she looked as if she had stepped straight out of one of Mr Alfonso's magazines Mirembe's restless gaze had seen in his shop. What did not synchronise with the splendour she radiated was the concerned look on her face.

The lady walked swiftly around the black car to support the gentleman whom Mirembe knew was her husband. Contrary to his radiant wife, he appeared ash-grey and much wrinkled. His black suit, which was very formal and had a bright star in his lapel, hung in folds around him. The only thing that shone from him, apart from the bright star, were his eyes. Mirembe knew from experience this was fever.

Her little heart went out to the man, but as her mother had forbidden her to come and greet them, she remained standing and watching in the shade of the hut. She was near enough to overhear the conversation between them.

"Mr and Mrs Mayor," her mother was saying, nervously wiping her hands on her clean apron, "what an honour to visit us. Please do come and sit in the shade."

"Thank you for the offer, Lwango, but we can only stay for a short while," the lady answered, still supporting her husband, who did look like he would love to sit in the shade. "We've only driven down here from Atura to ask if Mirembe could come with us?"

"K? Mirembe?" Her mother had a puzzled look on her hard face. "There must be a mistake, Madam Mayor. My daughter can't speak; she won't be of any use to you. However, I have four strong boys …"

The lady interrupted Lwango, "Really, we cannot stay long. My husband isn't well, you see. Would you grant me permission to take Mirembe with us? We've heard all about her exceptional gift for the sick, and you see my husband is …?" Her voice trailed off.

Suddenly seeing the benefit of her wayward daughter getting acquainted with good, rich people, Lwango signalled to Mirembe to come closer, which she timidly did. She already felt this couple had good hearts and they did not mean her any harm, but she was overwhelmed by their grandeur and the fact she was asked to sit with the sick gentleman.

"Hello, Mirembe," the lady said in a friendly manner. "I'm Mrs Kasozi and this is my husband Mr Mayor. Do you know who we are?"

Before Mirembe could answer, the gentleman said in a raspy voice, "Please, Georgina, can we make it short? I need to lie down."

His wife looked at him with a deep wrinkle of distress between her eyes and nodded, quickly gesturing to the young girl.

"Please sit in the back, Mirembe, and don't be afraid. I'll explain to you when we're driving back home."

She then settled her husband in the passenger's seat with a plaid around his legs although it was a blisteringly hot day, and quickly slipped behind the wheel.

To the mother, she called, "Don't know for how long now, but will tell Master Kevin to let you know!"

She did not hear the mother mutter, "Do keep her if you feel like it."

TO MIREMBE THIS was all so sudden and new that she did not know what to feel or think. It was her first time inside a car. She was almost too small to look out of the window, but she craned her neck and saw how they left the village with everyone looking at the car and her in it.

Then she felt the leather upholstery, caressing it softly with her fingers, and looked at the interior, the grey seats, the ashtrays in the doors and in the middle part, the coconut mats on the floor, the windows covered in red dust.

Mrs Kasozi threw a quick glance over her shoulder to reaffirm she was okay. "I have to keep my eyes of this bumpy road," she smiled, "but as soon as we're home and sit down with a nice cup of tea, I'll explain everything to you. Your grandma Sanyu told me you're such a special little girl and Chieftain Oidu asked the priest for an official name change for you. Did you know he did that?"

Mirembe did not know, but her heart swelled with pride. She was so happy with her new name. It fitted her like a glove and Kabonesa had been such an insulting one. For the time being, benumbed and overwhelmed, she just stared at the back of the heads of the couple upfront, wondering where these unusual people were taking her. They were more like the white folk she had seen in Atura during market day, with their fancy clothes and confident manner.

The further they got from home, the more anxious Mirembe became and she wanted to hum, but dared not for fear the woman would not let her. She was at their mercy now and her little heart cried in silence.

"Oh, so now I'm going to work for them like Emerald does for grandma. Maybe I can play with her some time."

For Mirembe it was clear as day she would never be allowed to go back to her family. She sighed, a mixture of relief and agony.

Chapter 3

THAT NIGHT, SLEEPING FOR the first time ever in a real bed, Mirembe was as unhappy as she could be. She prayed for a long time as she lay wide-eyed gazing at the fan whirring above her head.

"Please, Lord Universe, let me go home. I will be better to Mummy, and I will help my brothers any way I can," she urgently pleaded. "I will never glance at their homework and sit with every sick person that wants me. Please, let me go home to my folks and I'll be as good as gold. This house is not a place for a poor girl like me. I don't belong here."

But nothing happened while she ardently cried out to her best friend, Lord Universe.

Then Mirembe heard Mr Kasozi cough loudly a few doors down the corridor and soon after Mrs Kasozi cry out, "Come here, quickly, Master Kevin. Mr Mayor is unwell again!"

For a while Mirembe lay listening to the commotion in the corridor, wondering whether she needed to come out and offer her assistance, but she was still at an absolute loss as to what her function was in this household.

WHEN THEY ARRIVED at the end of the afternoon, a maid had brought her to this room and told her it was her bedroom. She was left there for at least two hours before Mrs Kasozi came in and sat down next to her on the bed.

"I am so sorry, Mirembe," she said after what seemed a terribly long silence. "I hope Abbo brought you tea and sandwiches in your room? I honestly wanted to come earlier, but the car ride had taken its toll on Mr Mayor."

When Mirembe nodded that she had been fed, the mayor's wife continued. "I know it seems very unjust and so egoistic to take you away from your family because I need you here."

She paused again, and Mirembe wondered if she was out of breath. Shyly, she cast a sidelong look at the stately lady next to her and, out of pure loneliness, put her little hand in hers. She had been so afraid alone in the room with all the quaint furniture and lacy curtains and pictures of big cities with bright lights on the walls that she would gladly have slipped into the strange lady's arms if she let her.

Mirembe had never felt so ill-at-ease and frightened in her entire life. She knew Mr Kasozi was dying and that that was why she was brought to this house, but this gentleman was so very different from the people in her village she had sat with. He was - what was he? - rich and important and like a grandfather she had never known. Her father's parents had died when he was young and Mirembe had never known them.

Mrs Kasozi felt the girl's awkwardness and homesickness and acknowledged it by squeezing her fingers softly,

"I know, my dear," she said and, although Mirembe did not know what she meant by 'knowing', they did seem to have an understanding. Strengthened by their touch the lady continued. "You're very special, Mirembe, and not just because your grandmother says so, but I've been watching you in Church on Sundays as well. You're in a different league. So, here's my plan. It's not that you will work for me or that you have to do any household chores. On the contrary, you're going to help me look after Mr Mayor and in return I'll teach you how to talk."

At this Mirembe looked up at her in amazement. There was no way she could talk. Everybody knew she could not, that she was mute. But that opinion did not seem to be shared by her new protector.

"Sh, sh," Mrs Kasozi shushed her. "I know you think it is impossible, but I believe you only need a little push and lots of love and encouragement."

Mirembe sighed; she would love to be able to talk and she was sure her mother would want her back if she could, so maybe this was going to be her way out of this problem. She would do as Mrs Kasozi told her to and then, possibly, she could go home to her family because that was all she wanted at that moment. She felt lonely and estranged in this beautiful mansion and longed for her mat on the hard, mud floor and the scoffing from her mother and cold-shouldering from her brothers.

As Mrs Kasozi got up and stretched herself, she added, "Now, Mirembe, I have to go and see to my husband again, but Abbo, whom you have already met, will come in in a little while to take you down to dinner. For today we will have you wear this old dress as I have no one on the staff of your height, but tomorrow you can go to Mr Anthony's shop with Abbo to buy some new dresses."

DINNER FOLLOWED, which had been a real ordeal with Mr Mayor coughing all the time and his wife fussing over him while nobody paid attention to Mirembe, who had no idea how to hold a knife and fork and eat from a white porcelain plate that was way too high up on the table while her chair was too low.

With all her might she tried not to spill anything on the white tablecloth, but it was in vain. First plopped a greasy potato, then a spoonful of fruit. With cheeks red, close to tears, Mirembe was grateful when dinner was over and Abbo took her back to the unfamiliar bedroom.

Unable to express herself, she could ask no questions and the maid had left her alone to undress and get into the strange bed. Only then the tears came and Mirembe forced herself to make plans to escape and return to her family.

Maybe it would be easier to find her grandmother's house first and ask grandma to convince the Mayor and his wife to let her go home.

This thought comforted the confused girl enough to fall asleep while silence returned on the corridor.

IN THE MIDDLE OF the night she was awoken by a rough shaking of her shoulder and Abbo whispering in her ear, "You must come, Miss Mirembe, Mr Mayor is not good, and Mrs Mayor asks for you. Here, put on your dress and come with me."

Sleepy and disorientated, Mirembe did as she was told and on shaky legs and bare feet followed the girl slightly bigger than herself to the end of the corridor. Her heart was racing, and she felt sweat pouring down her back as Abbo opened the door to the master bedroom.

The maid felt the hesitation in the little village girl, so she pushed her inside, saying, "You must go in, Miss Mirembe, you must go in."

The words sounded almost as a prophecy and often in later years Mirembe would remember them and repeat them to herself. "You must go in, Miss

Mirembe!" It would be her mantra every time she had to walk over that threshold and into the chambers of death.

But as an eight-year-old she was simply frightened as she entered the shaded room where everything seemed beige; the upholstering on the furniture, the curtains, the thick carpet on the floor and the huge bed with the sunken body of the mayor in it, even his wife sitting on a beige chair by his side.

The stately mayor's wife looked up as the girls came in and she instantly summoned Mirembe to her side. Without orders Abbo left and closed the door.

Mrs Kasozi got up and whispered, "You sit here, Mirembe, and I will sit on the other side."

Both females sat for a while in silence listening to the irregular breathing of the patient in the bed. He seemed asleep, but then he woke up with what looked like an electrical shock shaking his body and cried out, "Georgina, are you there?"

And she answered, "Yes, Henry, I'm here and so is Mirembe."

On hearing her name, the sick man turned his ashen face towards the young girl and the stare in his feverish eyes frightened her. But there also seemed to be some pleading in them and her soft heart went out to him, trying to find ways to alleviate his suffering and make him know everything would be fine. It was as if her eyes transferred her prayers to him and he suddenly sunk back into the heap of pillows, closing his eyes and breathing more evenly.

"You see?" Mrs Kasozi said in a hushed voice. "Your presence does him so much good. He is at peace now, just knowing you are here. And I am also so much better now you're here."

Although the words were meant to be friendly, they did not make Mirembe feel better and she was fighting against sleep. At some point she must have nodded off and she woke again when a big black man with white gloves carried her along the corridor and to the bed.

SOME HOURS LATER Mirembe woke again feeling bewildered; where was she and what was expected of her? Everything was so new here whereas at home all the days had looked the same. She now did not know if that was a good thing or bad thing and, as she always had only herself and her Lord Universe to consult, she took this time to lie in the soft white sheets with her wiry black curls un-brushed and tangled, and asked her only Friend what she should do.

Slipping out of the house to ask Grandma Sanyu to take her back to her family was now not as much at the forefront of her thoughts as it had been the evening before. The words Mrs Kasozi said to her about the comfort she brought had struck a chord with her. Finally someone had told her that she had a function in life and was not just a nuisance. And then there were the other things she had said about teaching her to talk and new dresses she could have.

It all sounded so exciting, but excitement was not a feeling Mirembe was familiar with. It made her ponder this new emotion; what it did to her and how she would act upon it.

"But what if I stay here and become part of this family," she thought to herself. "Daddy will miss me when he smells like that, but he's the only one. Still, they are my family, they know me best and they know I am no good. So, shouldn't I be returning to them to learn how to be better and they will love me? Mrs Kasozi is awfully nice, but I don't know her, and her husband is going to die in a couple of days. And then Mrs Kasozi will probably send me home anyway. She will forget all about teaching me to talk and I possibly cannot even keep the dresses she has promised me. But it is true that Mr Kasozi was lying ever so peacefully in his bed after I looked at him. I only did what I always do when people are suffering; I send them the love of the Lord Universe, the love that He tells me to give to them. I don't do anything, it's all His doing."

The confusion in Mirembe's mind went on until Abbo came to fetch her for breakfast. Nobody was in the large, luxurious breakfast room, a different room from where they had dinner the evening before. Only one plate was laid out on a white napkin on the mahogany table and Abbo gestured to her to sit down.

"Master Kevin will be coming soon to serve you your breakfast, Mirembe," Abbo said in an important voice. "After you have had breakfast, I will take you to the bathroom to have a bath and then we will go to Mr Anthony's shop for new dresses."

Mirembe nodded and sat down. She waited for at least ten minutes, sitting completely alone in the still room, peeping around and wondering where they had gone. At home there was always a cacophony in the morning and the little round space with seven people in it resonated with voices, so this peace and quiet was another new experience.

As always when she did not know what to do, she started humming to herself, and was surprised to hear herself utter some syllables that sounded something like "Here … I … am, I, I am here." She was so taken unawares by the words in her own voice that she put her hands over her mouth as if to silence herself.

At that moment the large black man with the white gloves who had carried her to her bed burst into the room balancing a tray with a silver-topped plate. With a large gesture, he put the silver-topped plate on top of the plate in front of her and removed the lid.

What Mirembe then saw made her open her eyes wide. There was a display of fine cubes of white bread with jam, a grapefruit with all its skin peeled off in small parts, a bowl of yoghurt decorated with raisins, and a small piece of cheese on a miniscule mat. Mirembe had never seen such food before and she did not know what it was, but as she looked up at the man everyone called Master Kevin, she saw him nodding at her,

"Go ahead, Miss," he said in his deep loud voice, clearly enjoying her startled look. "I'll bring in the tea and the fresh juice in a minute. It's all for you, so taste it good. And let me tell you that you have come to the right place. Mrs Mayor will never let you go hungry, or in lack of anything your little heart desires."

As he left the room, Mirembe looked at the display of food on the plate for a while until her hunger let her dive in. While chewing she was thinking of Kevin's words, wondering if she had landed in paradise.

THE REST OF THE day went by in the same state of amazement and puzzlement for the young, un-educated black girl from the village. She kept fingering the pink dress that fell so smoothly over her clean-washed knees and the matching pink ribbon in her hair.

She had not seen Mr and Mrs Kasozi all day, but Abbo told her they had appointments at the hospital and would be back in the afternoon. Mirembe was dying to be able to talk to the maid, who had been her companion for hours now and who seemed so natural and free in her behaviour. Abbo spoke of her employers with great pride and did not at all sound like a work maid.

Mirembe knew that the first thing she would have asked her was if Abbo knew where her Grandma Sanyu lived and whether they could go and visit her sometime. Mirembe also felt inadequate that she could not read or write as well as Abbo, who was also adept at adding and subtracting numbers.

"You have made a mistake, Mr Anthony," Mirembe heard her say. "Three dresses of 22 shillings is 66 shillings and not 69. You must not rip off Mr and Mrs Mayor, Anthony, or they will take their shopping elsewhere."

She had looked at the smart black girl with eyes full of admiration. This was how she too wanted to be, equally confident and honest. Mirembe wanted to be her friend and learn all Abbo could teach her.

Then she remembered that Mrs Kasozi had promised to teach her to talk and if it was anything like learning to read or to write, Mirembe was sure she would master all these skills at some point. The first words this morning had been a favourable sign. Maybe she was not as retarded as her mother told her and everyone else.

BOTH SHE AND HER benefactors were happy to see each other at dinner. For some reason the big dining room did not look as daunting as it had the night before. Mr Kasozi signalled her to come to his side and he gently caressed her head.

In his broken voice, he gasped, "Oh, Mirembe, this new dress suits you so well. What a precious little girl you are."

This gesture and his words made her feel awkward; he was a stranger after all and no one had ever said such friendly things to her, apart from occasionally her Dad when he smelled. Mr Kasozi smelled differently; he smelled of a different world, the world where the Angels sang, and Lord Universe was the Master.

Mrs Kasozi asked her how her day had been, and this made Mirembe stare at her with fear in her eyes, but then she remembered what she had been able to say that morning and courageously she said, "I … Am … Here." Her voice quivered, but the sounds were unmistakable.

Mrs Kasozi smiled. "Well said, Mirembe. And, yes, you are here! Bless you!"

THAT NIGHT MIREMBE slept like a rose and had a dream.

She walked in a meadow filled with flowers in different colours, yellow, red and blue, and they came up to her knees, wafting lovely smells into her nostrils. Strolling through the summer field with a clear blue sky above her, Mirembe realised she was in a different country, as nature was lush, all plants green as if they had recently been washed by the rain, a country without red mud.

On realising she was somewhere else, she panicked for a moment. Everything was so different from her African roots.

Then she heard a voice calling out to her in a kindly tone, "It's okay, Mirembe; you are not tied to the African soil. You were created out of red mud, but you aren't red mud. All these flowers, all these beautiful flowering plants are your people and you are here with them, but you're not owned by them. You can go your own way."

The Voice pushed her on as wind in her back and, as she strolled further and further into the field, the flowers turned into people waving at her and she waved back. She turned around to see if the Voice was still following, but it had retreated to the bushes bordering the meadow.

"I want to be able to talk to my people. I need to be able to talk, or I can't help them. Please help me talk, Lord Universe."

Her voice sounded as clear as the water of the Victoria Nile appeared, but the Voice didn't answer.

Yet Mirembe knew the answer in her heart and awoke with a smile.

Chapter 4

EVERY DAY MIREMBE WAS able to say more words, while Mr Kasozi's health deteriorated. It was a time of joy and agony; joy because her biggest wish was being granted, but agony because she became attached to her benefactors and knew she would have to say goodbye to one of them very soon. Especially seeing Mrs Kasozi suffering, who tried also to keep up her husband's role as Mayor of Atura next to seeing to his needs, broke the kind child's heart. In that last week of Mr Kasozi's life, the bond between the three of them was forged for eternity.

Mirembe's days swung from being filled with new tastes and adventures to tending to the mayor's final hours. She was too busy now to think of home, but home had not forgotten her.

When she was with the Kasozi's for four days and they were in the afternoon room making the patient comfortable on a long chaise, Master Kevin came in to announce Lwango was at the door. By this time Mirembe did not want to go home anymore, so she looked around with a frightened expression, wondering if she should hide somewhere. She was sure her mother had come to take her back.

Mrs Kasozi said, "Don't worry, dear, you stay here, and I will deal with your mother." And to Master Kevin she said, "See Lwango into the front parlour and I'll be with her in a minute."

Mirembe wanted to follow her, but Mrs Kasozi stopped her. Curious though about what her mother wanted, she sneaked to the door and listened in to the conversation.

She heard her mother say, "I have been wrong, you see, I need Kabonesa ... uh ... Mirembe home.

You must understand that I need another pair of female hands to look after five males?"

Then she heard Mrs Kasozi reply, "I do understand that, Lwango, but the type of help you need should not be provided by your daughter. You have no idea how special that girl is, and I am not going to let you waste her talents in house chores and getting her married off in her teens."

Her mother protested, stating that it was the sole reason girls were born and she did not want her daughter to get fancy ideas in her head that she could be anyone else but a housewife and a wife.

The discussion went on for a while and Mirembe started to doubt whether Mrs Kasozi had enough arguments to keep her here; after all, she was not her legal mother. Why the mayor and his wife had no children of their own was a mystery to the young girl. They seemed to really love children, especially girls, whereas her own mother only liked sons.

In the end the two women came to the decision that Mrs Kasozi would pay for a maid to help Lwango out for three days a week. Mirembe let out a big sigh of relief and quickly ran back to the afternoon room in case her mother found her at the door and took her with her against her wish.

When she entered the room, she realised Mr Kasozi was dying and quickly pulled the bell cord near the door to let Mrs Kasozi know she had to come quickly. Meanwhile she sat herself on a little stool next to the chaise longue and took the mayor's shrunken hand in hers.

His breathing was shallow but even and he kept his friendly gaze on her, fixing her eyes in his. Mirembe had done this before and was not afraid of death, but this was the first time she would help a human being over the threshold she had come to love. That made it more complicated for her, but she was firm with herself and told herself she could do this.

"Just let go, Mr Mayor, it will be all right, I'm here, so just go," she kept repeating silently and could see her unspoken words being transferred to him, and that he understood and concentrated on dying.

He was gone before his wife returned to the room still busy in her head with the argument with Mirembe's mother.

"Oh, my God!" she exclaimed when she saw what was going on. "Now my darling has gone without me being here. How terrible this is. I will never forgive myself. Oh, my darling, oh, my darling."

Cautiously Mirembe freed her warm hand from the dead man's quickly stiffening one and made her way to the grieving widow. She softly pressed her down in a chair and sat with her.

"It's okay, Mrs Kasozi," she said. "He died peacefully. It's okay."

"Oh, my God!" Mrs Kasozi cried. "Mirembe, dear, you are talking. What a miracle, what has happened?"

Mirembe looked at her and then realised she had spoken aloud the words she was thinking and that it was indeed a miracle. It had not been possible in all the years that lay behind her; she had only been able to formulate her thoughts in her head.

To check if it had not just been a one-time thing, she said, "No, Mrs Kasozi, from now on I will be talking as any other human being. Thank you so much for trusting in me."

"Please call me Georgina," Mrs Kasozi pleaded, her beautiful eyes full tears. "Henry was the only one to call me by that name and I want you to be as close to me as possible. Oh, my dear Henry. In a way I must be glad he is no longer in pain, but how I will miss him. Did you know we have been together for over forty-five years in marriage? Oh, my dear husband. And now he's gone and what is to become of me?"

Mirembe sat with the overwrought woman's hand in hers, all the while thinking what would happen to *her* now. Could she stay with this lovely lady, but in what role? She was only there for the dying.

Absorbed in her own thoughts, she did not hear Abbo come in, who had reacted to the pull on the bell cord. The shocked, loyal maid put her hands over her mouth and burst out in tears. She muffled them with her fingers, but her little shoulders shook.

Feeling it pulling on her heartstrings, the little girl immediately loosened her grip from the older lady and ran over to her new friend. Together they stood and then Mirembe's tears came as well. They cried their hearts out and the older lady joined them after a while.

It must have been a strange sight to Master Kevin, who came in to see what all the lamenting was about. When he saw his beloved master dead in the chaise longue, he too sobbed, and suddenly Mirembe understood that these people were real. They showed what they felt; they loved each other and cared for each other, were happy and sad for each other, and a flower bloomed in her heart until it almost burst with happiness through her tears.

Somewhere, somehow, she had always known there were people who had deep feelings and acted upon them; she had longed and longed for eight years to find them and now they were all around her.

"Death is strangely beautiful," she said to herself. "It brings out in people those deep, deep feelings of what life is really about and what we are able to share with each other. Only death can make us love each other this way. Isn't that strange? But it is as true as truth can be. I will never be without death in my life for long. It's a part of me."

BUT THOSE WERE ONLY momentary emotions. Soon the reality of having to bury the town's mayor and the arrangements that were needed to bring that about occupied everyone's thoughts and time.

Automatically, little Mirembe's concern had gone over from the sick man to his grieving widow and she would not let Georgina out of her sight during the day. It felt odd to address this great lady, who could be her grandmother, as such, but in order to service her even better, Mirembe pushed her timidity aside and dared to be bold enough to address Mrs Mayor by her Christian name as often as she could to show her willingness.

Being now very much part of this odd family that had basically consisted of the Mayor and his wife and their two servants, Mirembe had to get used to people in Atura looking suspiciously at her as she walked at Mrs Kasozi's side and was consulted about the colour of the flowers for the Mayor's wreath, and the Psalms to be sung at his funeral service.

Atura grew accustomed to having an unconventional, progressive Mayor, but never before had a poor girl from a hamlet on the Victoria River Nile been allowed to make decisions of that calibre. They could not find a reason against Mrs Mayor's choice, but many remembered the girl's mother Lwango and suspected some plot from that devious woman's mind.

Also, the fact that the mayor's wife was obviously in deep mourning and not herself, made some raise their eyebrows at the power the little girl was given and the more brazen ones talked about this unheard of situation behind their backs.

Mrs Kasozi, who had been the Mayor's wife for forty-five years, knew all the ins and outs of her people and was well aware of their glances and hidden remarks.

"Let them stare and talk, dear," she said, giving Mirembe's hand a little squeeze. "Only you and I, and Abbo and Master Kevin, know what the truth is and we are the only ones that really matter here."

"Are you the Mayor now, Georgina?" Mirembe asked.

"For the time being, yes, but there will be elections after the three month period of grieving is over. I think Mr Anthony would like to be the new Mayor and otherwise Mr Bwandale from the machine factory. But by that time we will be on our way to Europe, my dear."

Mirembe looked up at her with wild astonishment in her big eyes. "Europe? What is Europe, Georgina?"

Georgina just laughed and added mysteriously, "A place where ladies go that need a break."

Chapter 5

"WHEN'S YOUR FLIGHT again, Mir?" Georgina spoke to her through the open bathroom door, where she was clipping on her pearl earrings and making the final arrangements to her hair before they went out to celebrate Mirembe's graduation cum laude from Kampala International School.

"The day after tomorrow, Mam." Mirembe lay on Georgina's king-size bed, the one in which they had laid Mr Mayor to rest after he died from a double pneumonia ten years earlier.

While waiting for Georgina, she played with Kitty, their grey-haired Schnauzer, who ran around on the chintz covers trying to get hold of the piece of string Mirembe was pulling in front of her nose.

She had sincerely tried to call Georgina by her first name and continued to do so during their first months together, but while sipping lemon soda on the balcony of their hotel Palazzo Veneziano in Venice, they had both come to the conclusion that it made Mirembe too uncomfortable and 'Mam' would suit them both.

"Have you checked whether you can take both your small rucksack and your violin as hand luggage? You can't have the expensive instrument in the cargo hold. You know how they handle luggage at airports."

"Yep, it's possible."

Georgina, now in her early seventies, emerged from the bathroom, a little bent and thinner but still a beautiful, stately lady.

Her warm eyes took in the two young creatures on the bed and she uttered in mock annoyance, "Oh, Kitty, you naughty little thing. Mir has spoilt you rotten since she's been back! You know you're not allowed on the bed."

It was clear, though, she was all too happy to have them both under her roof again and the ruin of her expensive cover was the least of her worries.

"Let's go," she announced. "I've booked a table at that new restaurant on the waterside; I think it's called Namazzi's Bistro. Heard some good stories about it. It'll be just the four of us as in the old days; Abbo, Master Kevin and you and me. How proud Mr Mayor would have been of you. I wished he could have lived to see you excel at school as you did, but then again," she remarked, putting her arm through Mirembe's, momentarily looking quite sad, "you would not have been here at all, hadn't he died."

She sighed at the memory of bringing that sweet, dirty little girl into her house at the most difficult time in her life. What a comfort Mirembe had been to her and how her lovely, intelligent, always positive attitude had helped her through her bereavement. She would not have been able to come through that period as she felt now if it had not been for her adopted daughter. Feeling that she had been utterly selfish, taking the little girl from one European country to another in an attempt to cope with the pain of losing her lifelong companion, Georgina had decided upon their return to Atura in the spring of 1989 - Mirembe was nine years old and privately tutored for over six months - that it was time to stop thinking solely of herself and think of the girl's future. That future would be bright, of that Georgina had not a single doubt.

All these thoughts went through Georgina's mind, as her daughter who was now almost a head taller than her Mam gave her arm a knowing squeeze and they walked towards the kitchen where the other two people to the party were waiting.

Abbo, now in her twenties, still the slight black woman with a friendly almost childish countenance, had her hair in tresses of tiny braids tightly braided to her scalp that seemed to stretch her skin. She wore a flowery dress for the occasion and jumped into Mirembe's arms. The girls stood hugging for a long time. Abbo occasionally popped in to help Georgina when the latter was in residence in her

Atura house, but now being the mother of twin three year old boys and also busy in her husband's clothes store, she hardly had time to take on extra chores.

Master Kevin, a stern, greying man with an age difficult to detect, had not changed much and was now the only live-in servant. Although outwardly still his large and healthy self, his big head with the wide pores giving him the appearance of ever sweating, and wiry hair always clipped short, he seemed to have become even more reserved. For the occasion of going out he had taken off his white gloves and for the first time Mirembe saw his hands were covered in red eczema patches.

Her heart went out to him, but she instantly revived when he said to her in his loud, booming voice, "If it wasn't for Miss Mirembe, this house would not know the sound of voice. And you couldn't even talk when you arrived here as a little, broken wench."

Both always smiled when he spoke those words, but it was clear the loyal servant still missed his former master and the liveliness the little girl had brought into the house.

She suspected the aging servant was suffering from depression, and was extra kind to him when she was home and he appreciated that. She loved seeing the sun break through on his broad face every time he saw her, and Mirembe knew he wished for the days she had arrived as a frightened little girl and he could feed her his healthy dishes. To Master Kevin, she would always be that little girl. She had never heard him talk of his own family and assumed they were all dead. She dared not ask him and Georgina said she did not know either.

"Stone-faced when I bring up the subject of his family. It must be the war. He's from up North, you know," she had declared. "Poor Kevin, but at least he's happy in the small Kasozi household."

To Mirembe it was an absolute joy to be back - if only temporarily - in the house she had grown up in, although that was only occasionally after Mr

Mayor's death, as Georgina had first taken her on a long tour through Europe, before sending her to boarding school in Kampala. Summer holidays were often enjoyed in the family's beach house on Lake Victoria, where Master Kevin would also be shipped to, mumbling and grumbling that he did not like it there. Atura, however, was home like no other home. She agreed with Master Kevin on that.

Some part of her was sad she would have to leave again soon and leave behind what she regarded as her real family, as she was to fly to Ireland where she had been admitted to Trinity College for an undergraduate programme in psychology. Her kind heart was torn in two; on the one side she could not wait to start her new adventure in Dublin, and on the other hand she knew how homesick she was going to be for Atura and her loved ones.

Being so far away, in a cold and Northern country, she would only be able to come home for Christmas and during the summer vacation. Throughout the years at boarding school in

Kampala, she had at least been able to come home every two months and for special occasions, such as Abbo's wedding to Mr Anthony's son Gilbert, when she had been her bridesmaid.

Mirembe was now proud godmother to Benny, one of the twins, while Georgina held the same function to the other little boy, Gary.

Mirembe's thoughts rarely returned to the hut on the Victoria Nile River where her blood relatives lived. After the single feeble attempt of her mother to get her back and then gladly accepting the financial support Georgina had offered, Mirembe only saw her family in Church and this always led to an uncomfortable atmosphere on both sides.

Both parties had refrained from seeking contact and, despite occasional pangs of alienation and loneliness, Mirembe had settled into her city life like a duck to water, taking up violin lessons, riding her pony and excelling in hockey. She was an accomplished girl at eighteen, extremely beautiful and athletic, but still with the same kind heart that overflowed when people were in need.

She thought, though, that she had found a balance between her sensitivity and her happy, radiant self, as she had been sociable and popular at school, always in the middle of a group of giggling girls. There was no reason not to explore university life and embrace that fully.

These days, there was nothing Miss Mirembe could not do.

THEY HAD JUST SETTLED on the waterside of Namazzi's Bistro, sipping aperitifs, when a dirty, barefooted boy of around ten years old in torn shorts and a faded t-shirt came running up the steps of the patio.

"Are you Miss Kabonesa?" he asked, catching his breath.

It was clear he had been running for a long time. As nobody addressed her by her birth name anymore, certainly not after the priest had officially changed it in the Church annals, the four pair of eyes just stared at him, realising he must be from Mirembe's village.

The little boy was adamant. "Please, Miss," he begged, "it's your father. He's not well."

Georgina glanced at her daughter with a concerned look in her eyes. She knew too well how Mirembe reacted to such news and realised where the extra fidgetiness the girl had displayed all day came from. She had put it down to nervousness for her upcoming trip to Ireland and college life, but now she knew. Mirembe always sensed when something was going on in her circle.

Addressing the panting boy instead of her daughter, Georgina replied, "Do sit down, boy. I'll order a lemonade for you. Mir, what do you want? It's up to you, honey, you know."

"I have to go, Mam, I have no choice. I knew it. He wasn't looking well in Church. I'll have to go, but I have no idea how long it's going to last. Will I miss my plane?"

"This is how we shall do it," Georgina replied in a reassuring tone. "We'll take it a day at the time.

Lectures aren't starting for another three weeks. We have time and can always reschedule your flight. So, do what is best for you, but do take the car. I don't need it. Just see if you want to stay overnight or return later tonight. Take the boy with you."

"But, Mam, what about our festive dinner? I'm so sorry." She looked apologetically at Abbo and Master Kevin, but both waved her apologies away.

"We'll do it when you return at Christmas," Abbo assured her, "and we'll have something else to celebrate then as well." She proudly tapped her growing belly.

"Okay then," Mirembe agreed, "I'll be off. I'll take overnight things with me, but I'm not sure I'll be sleeping there. I really wouldn't know how to fit in anymore. I dread it like anything."

Chapter 6

NOT BEING AN EXPERIENCED driver yet, it took all Mirembe's attention to stay on the red mud road to get to her former hamlet. It was a good thing, she thought, that she had to concentrate so much, as she was full of trepidation for was at the end of the red road, the place where she had lived for eight years but had never returned to since.

She had no idea who the little boy was on the back seat still as a mouse and Mirembe did not feel like small talk. It had rained that day and the road was slippery. Red clots of mud spat against the windshield, making the road even more difficult to see.

It was pitch black outside Atura and only the headlights of the Ford, a newer version than the one she had sat in ten years earlier, were her only guidance.

Eventually she saw the semi-circle of huts raise up in the lights and people emerging from them, all in expectation of the prodigal daughter returning home. Had the girl who had been poor and retarded, but was now rich and well-educated, returned to help her father to the other side? It seemed that way.

Chieftain Oidu approached the car, as he felt he was in charge of the community, but waited until Mirembe stepped out.

Her silk shawl got caught in the evening breeze and slipped off her shoulders. She stood there in her festive, designer dress, this Paris' season, as she had not taken the time to change when she grabbed a few articles for the night and the car keys. Her black pumps with the high heels sunk deep into the red soil and she felt incredibly vulnerable and exposed.

No one spoke.

Her mother Lwango could be seen standing some distance back with the other women. Her four brothers, three married to girls from their community and other villages along the river, stood with Oidu. The little boy who had been in the car took advantage of all the confusion to slip back to his parents' hut and disappeared from sight.

Her eldest brother, Mukisa, eventually addressed her. "Dad is very ill and asked for you," he said simply, and both siblings felt a strange shock that he was actually speaking to her for the first time in their lives.

Mirembe nodded, momentarily feeling as if she was mute all over again, but then she said in her clear, musical voice, "Where is he? In our hut?"

She heard the whole crowd whisper in awe as she spoke and her eldest brother also startled but, recovering himself without answering, he beckoned her to follow him.

Mirembe felt every step she took, not just due to the impractical shoes she wore, but also because of all the eyes on her and in anticipation of what she would find once she entered her former home.

Before she could cross the entrance where Mukisa held open the cloth, Lwango approached in haste and put her hand on her daughter's silk sleeve.

"Did you bring any money?" she hissed. "He," and she pointed with her thumb into the semi-darkness of the hut, "needs a doctor. Now!"

Mirembe was taken aback by her mother's greeting after all these years, but slipped into her role of good daughter like a glove, and replied, "Yes, Mother, I have, as much as you need."

"Good," Lwango replied with a sly smile and Mirembe knew the money would not be spent on a man who had little use for medical care anymore.

It was time to reacquaint with her father, who still held a soft spot in her heart. "You must go in, Miss Mirembe," she told herself.

A SINGLE GAS LAMP flickered next to his mat and lit his dried-up face in yellow light, making him appear ghostlike and otherworldly. All the mats had been put on top of each other to give his emaciated body a little more comfort, but his eyes were open and alert.

"My child," he whispered, and tears flooded from his eye sockets, disappearing in the folds of his wrinkles and reappearing near his mouth.

He stretched out a thin arm with the flesh hanging from it like sheets in the wind. Mirembe's eyes also filled up and her heart was about to burst. Not thinking of high heels or expensive dresses anymore, she sank on her haunches next to her father and embraced him. The smell reminded her of Mr Mayor, the beckoning smell of Lord Universe, and the girl could not control herself. Years of pent-up loneliness and longing for her kind-hearted father made her break down, if only for as long as she allowed herself to.

She knew what she had come to do, and she would do it as she always did.

"How are you feeling, Dad?" she asked, putting a soft, cool hand to his dry forehead.

"Oh, to hear your voice for the first time," the sick man said with as much passion as he could muster, "and what a beautiful voice you have, my daughter."

The other family members had retreated to give them time alone and soon father and daughter were telling each other all that had happened in their ten years apart. Mirembe spoke much more than her father, as his life had been the same monotonous string of days and years as she had known them to be. More humiliation from his wife, more catching fish and drinking Waragi. Her life, on the other hand, sounded almost too exotic for her father's old ears, yet he listened with all his attention, nodding and smiling continuously. After they had talked for hours, he fell asleep with a contented glow on his spent face.

While the gas lamp sputtered, she listened to her father's breathing and attempted to come to terms with being in the old hut again, feeling her timid self return in not knowing what was expected of her right now.

All the fibres in her body wanted to jump back into that car and race to her safe, lovely life in Atura. She did not look forward to staying in the cramped place for much longer. The vibe she got from her mother was not inviting and she had to admit she loathed the dirt and simplicity of it all.

Trying to make up her mind and thinking intently of her dad, she dozed off, leaning against the pile of mats on which her father lay.

She awoke when she felt tugging on her arm and realised her mother was trying to grab the handbag she still had around her shoulder. Seeing her daughter open her eyes and pulling her arm back in alarm, Lwango scurried away, but not before giving her daughter an ugly look.

Mirembe sat up in a flash, staring at her mother in fear and disbelief. Why? She had told her she would give her the money, so why steal it from her? The two women gazed at each other wordlessly until her mother retired to a dark corner in the hut.

HANNAH FERGUSON

Mirembe turned around to see to her father, but to her perplexity realised he was dead.

His death had been a beautiful one, as there was a large smile on his face, showing the pink gums of his toothless mouth. She knew, despite her grief and turmoil, that all was good now and that she was given permission to go and live her own life.

"Thank you, Dad," she said with tears in her eyes, "thank you for everything." Turning to her mother, she said, "Thank the Lord Universe, for your husband, my father, has died. I will return now to Atura, but tomorrow morning I will send a hearse to have him taken to his last resting place. I will bury him in Atura's graveyard under the willow next to the Church. Good bye, Mother."

Getting up, she realised this was the first and probably the last time her mother would hear her voice. Who knew what the future held, after all? In great dismay over the loss of her father and the greed of her mother, she did not look back.

She got into the car and drove away.

ONLY WHEN SHE WAS on the plane to Dublin did Mirembe allow her thoughts go back to that sudden return to her birthplace and to the sad yet beautiful leave she had taken of her father. She knew well that the visit to the hut had unsettled her. That event combined with the new adventure awaiting her in a strange, foggy country, which took her far away from everyone she knew and loved, suddenly overwhelmed the eighteen year old. It unhinged her and made her feel extremely thin-skinned and unsure.

Ten years of advanced education and the best of everything had helped to bury her insecurities deeply in her soul, so deep that she herself was convinced they no longer existed, but one encounter with her hostile mother and her now deceased father had ripped open old wounds.

Who was she? What did she pretend to be? Had she become too proud, too self-assured?

Mirembe thought of her violin above her head and how she always picked up the instrument when she felt alienated from her surroundings, and how the lyrical sounds and the feel of that tender instrument under her chin and the soft strings moving over the snares calmed her.

"I will play a lot in Dublin," she promised herself, "every time I feel like this."

By the time she arrived in overcast Dublin, shivering in her thin African coat although it was only the end of August, most of her sensitivities had subsided again, at least for the time being, and she approached her new life as the strong, young woman she also was, looking forward to college life, new friends, new knowledge and new adventures.

Chapter 7

MARTIN DEBECKER HAD BEEN circling around her for a couple of months and although Mirembe thought the Dutchman attractive, tall and blond like a surfer, she was also ill-at-ease with him. He had intense eyes, blue like marbles, and when he fixed his gaze on her, she felt she could not escape anywhere. He had a catlike manner of walking, as if he would jump on her. It reminded Mirembe of a tiger she had seen in Kampala Zoo, pacing to and fro in front of the gate, when Mam had taken her there for her tenth birthday and she had suddenly started crying.

"He's so-so scary, Mam, I don't want to see him," she cried, putting her chubby hands over her eyes not to see the predator.

It had taken a double ice cream to soothe her and coax her back into the park to watch the other animals.

Mirembe went to an all-girls boarding school and was considered too well off to go out with the boys that hung in the streets of Atura waiting to pick up a local girl, and therefore had no experience with boys whatsoever. Boys were unknown territory to her. Like the tiger, she found them rather scary.

She had also never considered what type of boyfriend she would like, African of white, but having been at Trinity College for almost a semester, she understood romantic alliances between college females and males were formed and dissolved on a regular basis; it was almost like a game one played for fun and distraction - boyfriend, girlfriend, single again. It was part of the life she now led and she understood she had to experience romance herself to become fully part of this phase.

When Martin asked her out to a rugby match, she therefore said yes, not because she liked rugby or him very much, but because she thought this was how you started a relationship with the other sex.

"WANT ANOTHER BEER, Mir?" he shouted over the noise on the field below, but she shook her head.

She was not accustomed to much alcohol and had already had two drinks. Martin shrugged and got himself a straight vodka with his new beer. A sudden flashback to her father overcame her, but Mirembe suppressed it. As far as she knew, all men drank a fair amount of alcohol. What did worry her was that he was driving later, yet drinking at a high pace.

Not enjoying the match or his disinterested company - Martin chatted with a fellow student from his class all the time - Mirembe decided she wanted to go home.

"I'd like to go," she said just after the break started before the second half.

He still had paid no attention to her and she was afraid Martin would get too drunk to drive. She was sure he would not let her drive his new two-seater BMW.

"Okay, hon," he agreed good-naturedly, flipping his blond lock of hair out of his face as was his habit and giving her his intense blue stare.

Raising himself to his six-foot-two length and slapping his pal on the back with a 'see ya!' he grabbed her arm and pushed her rather roughly before him to the exit.

As soon as they sat in his car, he leant over to kiss her, but Mirembe was so out of sorts she pushed him away.

"Okay, hoity-toity black Ma'am", he grumbled indignantly, starting the engine and taking off at much too high a speed. "Where too, Cold Princess?

"Home, please," Mirembe answered in a small voice.

"Oki-doki, Lady mine, but let's grab some takeaway on the way."

This was not what she wanted and yet she went along with it.

IT WAS THE FIRST time she let Martin come to her dorm room on the Trinity campus and it made her extremely nervous and anxious. He stood there, a giant of a man looking around at her African trinkets and posters on the wall, the violin in its case and the music stand, before letting his eyes rest on her single bed with the patchwork plaid Mam had bought her in Trinidad.

She held their takeaway curry, still with her coat on, feeling how this stranger overtook her life and her room, which had been her safe place until now.

They did not even eat the meal then - only later when it was cold - for he took to her bed immediately. This first time was not a pleasant affair for the shy, overwhelmed virgin; there was a lot of tugging and pulling on clothes and his weight on top of her was uncomfortable and hurt her. Martin was not a kind or considerate lover, more offhand and in a hurry. He did not even seem to notice it was her first time and did not ask if she was okay.

May be as well, she thought, or she would have burst out in tears.

Nothing was as she had hoped and while they were eating the cold curry she felt dirty and lonely. Martin did not mark any of this; on the contrary, he was in the best of spirits and entertained her with stories of his childhood in Amsterdam and his crazy entrepreneurial dad who would wake him in the middle of the night to go fishing, or skydiving.

"My dad was my hero, you know," Martin said through a mouthful of yellow rice. "I've never met a guy like him in all my life and never will. It's a damn pity he died last year." He wiped his mouth and dove into the mild yoghurt sauce with his finger.

Mirembe, still numb from their lovemaking, sat up somewhat, thinking she ought to ask how his dad died, but Martin did not need any encouragement.

"It was a freak accident. He was in one of his warehouses on the canal and wanted to check the stock on the top gallery. He just fell, three storeys down, and dead he was. Instantly! The doctor said it was a heart attack, but my step mum keeps saying he was depressed. I don't know what to think. I know he had a bit of a wild streak - just like me," and here Martin laughed rather unpleasantly, "and he could go through periods of feeling low. Well, anyways, I miss him a lot and now I'm the one who has to take over his businesses, and that's why I'm rushing through my MBA here at Trinity. Did my undergraduate programme in Amsterdam, but got sick of the place after my dad was gone and needed a breath of fresh air, and look who I bumped into? If that wasn't my luck. A real African queen. Heavens, I love your skin, it smells like exotic flowers."

He brought his rather large nose to her bare arm and sniffed deeply. "Never had a black woman before, though. Don't think the folks at home will be too pleased if I show up with you, but I couldn't give a damn. At least, not at this moment. Come, let me have you again!"

Mirembe dreaded the idea of repeating that painful exercise, but did not know how to stop him, so gave in.

AFTER THREE DAYS of the same she was so sore and miserable that she locked her door and let Martin bang on it for a repeated time. She stayed under her Mam's quilt pretending to be asleep, which was rather unbelievable with his loud exclamations and knocks. She would wait for the janitor to remove 'the gentleman' as they always referred to the male visitors to the girls' dorm. Mirembe was meanwhile terrified of missing classes and getting behind in her studies.

A day later, she was in so much pain that she had to crawl out of her bed and drag herself to the doctor. She had a massive bladder infection and was given medication that completely upset her system.

Her intestines emptied themselves and her head was either made of cotton wool or hurt so much she had to take painkillers not to pass out. Her entire body was numb, and she was slipping away, only she did not know where to. In her despair, Mirembe thought of buying a ticket home, never to return to Dublin so as not to have to see Martin again.

Mid-winter had arrived and the cold and humidity of the climate got into her bones. It was the lowest period of her life, she thought, as Martin kept banging on her door. Things could not get worse, she was sure.

How wrong she was.

MARTIN WAS NOT ONE to take no for an answer and he returned every day, coaxing her to open the door and let him in. Blurry-eyed and weakened from diarrhoea and not eating properly, Mirembe finally capitulated. Martin stood there with a huge smile on his handsome face and a grocery bag full of fruit and cookies in his arms.

He had even brought flowers.

With his usual vigour, he set out pressing oranges for her and making tea. For a moment, Mirembe was glad to have him in her life, but when he sat next to her on the bed and stroked her arm, she attempted not to cringe openly. Although not a tactful person at all, he did realise she was too ill to have sex and let her off the hook that day.

Mirembe desperately wanted to end the relationship, but had no idea how.

As soon as he made one friendly gesture towards her, she considered herself unkind and selfish if she did not let him have his way with her.

No matter that she studied psychology and had learned to be a proud and intelligent woman, in the first months of her relationship with Martin Mirembe shrivelled up completely and again became the helpless daughter at the mercy of a cruel mother.

She had no one to confide in. When she made her weekly phone calls to her Mam, she made sure she only told upbeat stories, as she did not want her elderly benefactor to find out and worry that her adopted daughter for whom she had done so much was actually making a complete mess of her student life.

IN THE SPRING MATTERS became even worse. Mirembe was skipping classes most weeks and lost a lot of weight. She was a shadow of herself, secretly hoping that by losing her looks Martin would back off and find a prettier girlfriend.

He kept returning, although he regularly also mentioned a red-haired Suzy. Mirembe did not ask any questions, but prayed to her Lord Universe that he would go to this Suzy and no longer bother her.

What she did not know was that she had become his prey and the more subdued and frightened she became, the more he enjoyed keeping her small. He occasionally gave her a slap on the buttocks in the past, but now the beatings were regular and not only on her behind. Unpredictably, for no reason at all, he would lash out at her.

"Black bitch, I've told you not to caress my back. The scar I have there from my first car accident hurts when the weather is like this."

He would hit her hard with his palm on her face. Mirembe would wince, clenching her teeth not to cry.

Another time she was trying to read an article on child psychology, but her mind kept wandering off. Martin came in and looked at her with an angry expression. Mirembe recoiled, but was too weak to get up and defend herself.

Lately the racial abuse was the new ingredient.

"You black cunt," he thundered and as he came nearer Mirembe smelled the alcohol on his breath, "what have I told you? You make sure you're ready when I come in or I'll teach you how to get ready."

He swayed on his feet, much drunker than he at first appeared. His once handsome face contorted; he moved his arms through space as a mad Don Quixote would. Mirembe glanced at the door, which was still ajar, calculating if she could slip past him and into the corridor and run to the janitor's office downstairs.

In his sly drunken state, he saw through her and, kicking the door closed with his boot, was on her.

Blows rained against her temples and her breast and he pulled her across the floor to her bed, all the while punching and mishandling her. Mirembe tried in vain to protect her head against the blows, but he was much stronger and much angrier.

"Black slut, I hate you, you black, black, black slut," she heard him scream as he was on top of her, pinning her arms and ripping off her clothes.

That was the last she remembered.

Chapter 8

SHE WAS IN A simple apartment in New York City. The one-room flat only had a bed, a table and chair, a mini kitchen in the corner and one small window with a lattice curtain that looked rather stained and yellow. Oddly, in the room there was a lot of baby stuff; a little crib, clothes, toys and a pack of nappies. On the bed sat a young woman with a dead baby in her arms, staring vacantly into space, motionless, emotionless.

Mirembe approached her cautiously and sat next to her on the single bed. "Give him to me," she murmured. "It's okay; you can give him to me."

But the young woman, who had a mass of dyed hair and a narrow face with grave eyes, refused to give Mirembe the dead child, so she just sat there next to the grieving mother, singing softly.

They sat side by side for a long time and Mirembe knew the girl's name was Annika, that she originally was from Arkansas, and that she was twenty-three years old and became pregnant after a one-night stand, but decided to keep the child despite her circumstances.

Annika was a secretary with a small book binding firm and lived on a modest salary. Still, she bought everything new for the baby and made plans to make things work for her and the child. The downstairs neighbour promised to look after the baby when she had to go to work.

The baby died the second day after its birth, and Annika's life was shattered. She was beyond tears, numb, frozen, in deep mourning.

Mirembe stayed with her for three days, arranged the funeral and helped the grieving mother get rid of all the baby things in her room.

The two women hugged and cried for a long while. Mirembe had to promise Annika she would come back, or the white woman would not let her go.

ON OPENING HER EYES, Mirembe realised she was in a hospital. Her body hurt, and it was impossible to move her head without becoming giddy. She also realised she had an out of body experience. Everything seemed so real, as if she was actually in New York and Annika from Arkansas with her dead baby had really been in her life. It did not confuse her in the slightest, but being in the hospital did. How had she ended up here? What had happened?

Slowly, through her bruised brain, the recent days came back to her and the way Martin had abused her. Concussion, ribs broken, dislocated shoulder, torn vagina and bruises all over that made her beautiful brown skin turn into a bluish-purple.

How on earth had she let that happen?

There and then, still physically weak, Mirembe decided, *No more Martin, now or never!*

AS SOON AS SHE was well enough to leave the hospital, she went to the police to report the abuse and the rape. She finally was not afraid of Martin DeBecker anymore. He was out of her life for good and she would see to it that he received his punishment.

Mirembe kept this promise. Martin was sentenced to six months in prison and a restraining order to never contact her again was issued.

Now, it was time to work on her self-esteem.

WHEN SHE KNOCKED for the first time on the door of Dr Tessa McGuiver, psychiatrist, old fears almost made Mirembe run, but having promised herself never to become the victim of another human being ever again, she pushed open the teak door and went in.

Behind the desk sat a woman, in her thirties, with a mass of gold-red curls and a kind, happy countenance on her freckled, almost transparent face. She looked up at her new client, a twinkle in her light blue eyes, and nodded, appearing nowhere near a psychiatrist as Mirembe had imagined one.

She felt an instant liking for this almost skinny, translucent and nymph-like woman. She had seen so many similar women throng the streets of Dublin, still fully embodying their Celtic past. Dr McGuiver was even wearing the national green in an expensive yet simple Irish sweater.

Walking around her desk, she made a wide, inviting gesture to the two comfortable white leather chairs near the window overlooking the Liffy River.

Showing two rows of perfect teeth, she smiled. "So, you must be Mirembe Kasozi, although I understand from your introduction letter that both these names were given to you during your childhood years and not from birth?"

The hand Mirembe shook was warm and strong and she could not help smiling herself. "Yes, and I'm again in a bit of an identity crisis, I'm afraid."

"Nothing we can't work out," the doctor said confidently, "and let's please call each other by our first names, if you can agree to that? I'm a strong believer therapy won't work when there's an artificial distance between therapist and therapy-seeker. I also hate the word 'patient'." Tessa smiled again, showing her beautiful teeth.

Mirembe instantly felt at ease and knew she came to the right place. It almost felt as if she had found a new friend.

"Coffee, tea, a soft drink?" Tessa asked, arching her eyebrows high and kicking off her high-heeled pumps.

"Tea, please; no milk, no sugar," Mirembe said gratefully, watching the thin-hipped therapist skip over her woolly rug on her stockinged feet to a small kitchen unit in the corner of the large office.

"I myself am totally addicted to black coffee," Tessa laughed. "One of my very few bad habits."

"I've never liked coffee," Mirembe said. "I know it's very un-African, but I just don't like it."

"Oh, I love it that you're African," Tessa sighed as she put down the cups and let her slender frame fall into the chair. "I've told Paul, my husband, that we should go to Kenya, or maybe Uganda, but I haven't got him that far yet. Well, one day, for sure! So, you must tell me all about it, because I want to know all about Uganda and about you and what makes you tick."

Mirembe liked her even more.

Tessa continued, "But enough small-talk. That's not what you're here for. What happened to you is serious and if you're up to it, please tell me about it. But let me first ask you if you are physically healed now?"

Mirembe nodded.

"And your attacker is safely behind bars?"

She nodded again.

"But he won't remain there and although he has a restraining order against him, we know these types of angry, uncontrolled young men might seek out their victims again. There are two things we must do. One," and Tessa raised a slim finger in the air, "make sure you become so strong mentally and spiritually that you will never be prone to such predators again, and two," and extra finger went up, "that he can't find you. As we have a couple of months, I would like to start with the first part; getting you stronger."

Tessa continued looking straight at her, light-blue eyes unwavering and strong. "I understand you have a very good and trusting relationship with your adopted mother, but you haven't told her anything about all this."

Mirembe shook her head, feeling small, seeing her lovely, elderly Mam before her eyes and missing her terribly.

"Good, we have to sort that out first," the doctor stated. "I understand this is difficult for you, but it has to be done. You cannot heal if you keep such a terrible thing from those that love you. So, I have a proposition to make. Is your adopted mother still able to travel?"

Mirembe nodded, feeling as if she had returned to her childhood muteness.

"Right, then I think the best course of action would be to invite her to come to Dublin and discuss your present state here in my office, the three of us together. How does that sound to you?"

Mirembe's heart, which had been so down-trodden and unhappy of late, jumped at the idea of seeing her beloved Mam and having this friendly doctor help breaking the terrible news to her.

Chapter 9

FOR MIREMBE'S GRADUATION summa cum laude as a Child Psychiatrist from Trinity College, a party was in order. During her two year therapy with Dr McGuiver she decided to change studies and opt for medicine first and then specialise in child psychiatry. When she understood how her early childhood experiences and the overnight change from poverty and neglect to wealth and love had influenced her, she knew she wanted to help children also struggling with life, in particular young African women with such a long way to emancipation before them.

Much had happened since Mirembe arrived as an innocent, susceptible freshman ten years earlier. She had been living with Paul and Tessa McGuiver for almost eight years now, having a whole apartment to herself on the second floor of their huge house on the Liffy River and every summer the three of them visited Mam at her summer house on Lake Victoria, after which Tessa and Paul would go on safari in Kenya or wild water rafting in Mozambique or hiking in South Africa.

Having arrived early at Dublin Airport, she was all excited to see her Mam. With four months of incredibly hard work on her thesis Treatment of Traumatic Stress Disorder in Infants and Young Children, she had thus had little time for phone calls or other social behaviour. Mirembe stood skipping from one foot to the other, but when her Mam finally appeared, slowly coming towards her through the doors to the arrival hall, she realised her beloved adopted mother was old and ill.

Georgina Kasozi, now in her eighties, was virtually a cripple. Rheumatism and arthritis had made her shrink almost a quarter of her former self, but being a proud woman she refused to sit in a wheelchair, and still walked with the aid of a stick.

Mirembe's eyes filled with tears as she enveloped tiny shoulders in her broad arms and kissed her.

Georgina looked up at her daughter with moist eyes full of admiration and, holding on to her for strength and support, exclaimed, "Oh, my dear, dear Mirembe, how proud Mr Mayor would have been of you!"

She pointed her stick to the high ceiling of the airport and looked up as if she was really seeing him there, a playful smile around her lips in their customary ruby-red lipstick. Other travellers looked at the two colourful African ladies, one young and strong and one frail and old, noting the unbridled happiness and love they spread, and found themselves involuntarily smiling too.

IT WAS A GOLDEN week for Mam and Mirembe in Dublin. The highlight was the graduation ceremony at the School of Medicine of Trinity College, where Mirembe Kasozi received much praise, and thereafter the great party at the McGuivers'.

All the while, though, Mirembe was aware she was about to say goodbye to her Irish years, as she had decided to return to Atura with her Mam. If she listened to her own heart, she would have wanted to accept the university's invitation to continue her PhD in trauma related child psychiatry, and only then set up her practice in Kampala, but for now she knew Georgina needed her.

Tessa and Paul were also shocked on seeing the declined health of the always so fragile but robust old lady. For them too it was a farewell party of mixed feelings. The McGuivers kept stressing they would come over for Christmas, but both wondered if it would be the last time to see Georgina.

FOR THE FIRST TIME in her life, coming home to Atura was a deception for Mirembe.

Of course, Master Kevin was still there tending to her needs and Georgina had hired a replacement for Abbo, twelve year old Michelle, who was actually Mirembe's niece as she was Mukisa's eldest daughter.

From their first meeting Mirembe took an instant dislike to the girl, who not only physically resembled her grandmother Lwango, but also had much of her way of acting. Michelle had a sly, underhand way of talking and moving around, trying to do all her tasks as quickly and as inefficiently as possible to then go off and gossip with her friends down the road.

Georgina seemed blissfully unaware of the girl's indolence and kept singing her praises. This also irritated the young psychiatrist, who could find no right way to open her mother's eyes.

Everything seemed to conspire to make it difficult to settle back into life in a small provincial town in Africa.

Her only comfort was schnauzer Kitty, whom she took for long walks and to whom she confided her disappointment and loneliness.

Life in Dublin, after its initial rocky start, had suited Mirembe, and she missed the big city life she had enjoyed to the brim. She also missed the opportunity to fly to London or New York for a couple of days just to sniff some culture or go on a shopping spree. And then there had been the psychiatry conferences in Zurich and Singapore. That was life! That was living! But most of all she missed her sophisticated friends and all the topics under the sun they had discussed with a glass of red wine in the pub or sipping crystal clear water while soaking in someone's Jacuzzi. From trans-genders to buying a ticket to go to Mars, it had been such fun and so invigorating.

Nothing had changed in Atura in the past ten years and it would probably remain the same for the next fifty. As the people there had always been far enough from the civil war that had plagued the country since Mirembe's birth, there was no reason for change, because only war seemed to be the hiccup for change in Africa.

Day in day out, the young woman - so full of life and accustomed to a different lifestyle - was as bored as a kid sitting in an empty room. Every day was the same. Georgina would wake late, way after ten, and then they would breakfast together in the breakfast room that still had the same pink-roses wallpaper that had been there the first day she walked in. Georgina ate little, half a boiled egg and two bites of toast, but she was happy to sit and chat with her daughter, never seeming to notice how dissatisfied the latter was.

She did profess it with words, saying, "I feel so selfish keeping you here with me in Atura when you have a career waiting for you."

But she knew Mirembe would wave her apology away and she was content with not acknowledging it further. Deep in her heart, Georgina felt she had a reason to be selfish. Her life would soon be over and, although she had never constrained her adopted daughter in any way, now that she would inherit her and her late husband's fortune she wanted to have Mirembe near in her last months of her earthly life.

She had sacrificed so much in not claiming her before, so that her adopted daughter could have the career she, Georgina Bigombe, daughter of a small merchant from nearby Buyala, never had. It seemed fair to ask that small favour and she was right, of course.

THE DAYS DRAGGED INTO weeks and weeks into months and Mirembe felt more discontented and apathetic every day. She picked fights with Michelle over nothing and the maid became more insolent as the young mistress's harsh words landed on her head. Sometimes Mirembe wondered if she had become a completely different person, cancerous and ugly, but she could not help lashing out at the girl, although she knew it would change nothing and she should constrain herself.

The only pleasures she had were her walks with Kitty and eating Master Kevin's healthy dishes. Conversations with Georgina became less and less as the old mistress retired to her bed most of the day.

Mirembe put on a lot of weight and that also made her crabby. She felt that at twenty-eight she was missing out on everything her peers were experiencing, starting their professional careers and getting ahead in life.

On other days she would scold herself, reminding herself that she owed everything to the Kasozis and that she should be eternally grateful and happy for everything she had. Those days she was extra nice to Michelle, knowing how easily she herself could have been in the shoes of this ill-fated girl. Michelle was fortunately in a better position than most of her family, as Georgina always sent her maids to school, making sure they learnt the basic skills of reading and writing.

MIREMBE SAT IN the windowsill with a book that had slid from her lap, staring at Georgina's beautiful Victorian garden where Master Kevin, who was almost as old as his mistress, watered the hydrangeas and pottered around in the vegetable garden with his eternal white gloves becoming more and more soiled.

It was a hot day, no different from any other day in Uganda's summer, but it felt different and Mirembe knew why. The day had come, the day she had dreaded so much, but also - if she admitted it to herself - had longed for.

The time had arrived for her Mam to join Mr Mayor.

As always death gave her intensely mixed emotions. Having experienced helping people over the threshold since she was a young girl, Mirembe dealt with death in a different manner than most. The hours before death were hard work for her; she concentrated all her attention on the dying person and gave them soothing messages for the transit.

Only in her father's case had it been different, for she had fallen asleep, but she was sure that Lord Universe had made the passage for her father soft and bearable even without his daughter's conscious help.

Sitting in that windowsill she was already present in Georgina's bedroom, where the beige curtains were drawn, and soft Vivaldi music played from her sound system. Kitty lay on the chintz cover close to her mistress, snoring softly. Georgina was on her back, fast asleep, but her hands with the deformed knuckles where arthritis had hit her hardest fumbled the cover.

At times she talked in her sleep, saying things such as "Henry, darling, you shouldn't wear white trousers to a committee meeting." Kitty changed positions when her mistress talked, but instantly fell asleep again, until the next disturbance. "Mirembe, sweetheart, hurry up, the ferry to Long Island won't wait forever."

Now and then Master Kevin popped his big, solemn head around the door that was kept ajar night and day, but seeing the mistress was slumbering he retreated again to find solace in his garden or his kitchen. For him Mirembe felt most sorry; he had been with the family since he was a young boy and had no idea what his position would be when the mistress died. She knew he knew she was not going to stay in the house for long, but for sure she would let him continue to live there. The unspoken words hung in the air between them and made both apprehensive.

Mirembe sighed. She really ought to go up and sit with her mother, but something held her back. This was going to be the most difficult task in her life, letting her beloved Mam go. Every fibre in her being fought against it and suddenly she realised why she had been so unhappy in the past months.

The boredom and the lack of work had only been a cover-up for this feeling she could not, would not face. Tessa had taught her how to analyse herself and yet at this most important moment in her life she had missed it. She could not let her mother go; there would be no one left when Mam was gone, no on who would truly love her and look after her. She was terrified of that prospect.

Placing her hot forehead against the cool window, she whispered in agony, "Mam, Mam, Mam."

I must let the tears come now, she thought, *before I go up and do what I have to do. There can be no tears, because then Mam will not be able to go. She won't, she will want to stay with me when she sees me in tears. It is hard enough for her to leave me here and go without me, so I must make it is easy as possible for her. But how on earth am I going to do that? Lord Universe, you must help me because I feel so afraid and so helpless.*

The sunrays fell across her worried face and she interpreted it as a caress and a sign she would be helped. Getting up slowly, she put the book on the side table and stretched herself.

"You must go in, Miss Mirembe!"

IN FACT, EVERYTHING she had fearfully anticipated did not happen. Georgina had already slipped into a coma from which she did not regain consciousness.

Mirembe sat next to her bed for the three days that remained of her Mam's earthly life and later recalled it as actually being the easiest transit she had ever helped with. While sitting there stroking her silent Mam's hand, she played their last conversation through her mind repeatedly.

"What else do you need from me, dear Mirembe?"

"Nothing, dearest Mam, you've told me everything."

"So, you go to my accountant Mr Alexander first and foremost when I'm gone?"

"I will, Mam, but let us please not talk of that now."

"I know, sweetheart, but we have to. I don't want matters to remain unsaid, especially not the boring business things that matter so much."

Mirembe had hung her head, but listened dutifully how rich she would be and what was expected of her to do with the inheritance.

Georgina was thorough when it came to business and she had always managed her affairs perfectly.

Mirembe, who had no economic knowledge whatsoever, as it did not interest her in the least, promised she would look after everything and consult Mr Alexander when she did not know what to do.

Her mother was not satisfied with her tepid reaction.

"Sweetheart, do listen to me! Money is important. It has made us do all these wonderful things together, all our travels, and remember how it got you to where you are now. I know you will be a famous psychiatrist one day. Knowing you will never have to worry about money makes me lay down my head in peace. But I must be convinced that you take it seriously, too. You see, money can also slip away from you so easily. You really have to keep an eye on it and I know what a softie you are, so there will be vultures after you to take advantage of you. Mr Alexander knows this as well, so please consult him always and never just give money away to someone who asks."

"No, Mam, but can we please now talk of something else? Would you like a cup of chamomile tea?"

"That will be lovely, my dear. You are right, I keep rambling on about money when we should take the time to enjoy each other's company. That's much more important."

Her Mam had been tired and had fallen asleep instead, the tea half drunk.

Were those really the last words they exchanged, Mirembe thought as she kept on stroking the thin dark hands with their swollen veins.

She realised the conversations between them had never really been about emotions, what they felt for each other. That hung in the air between them, unspoken, merely expressed in words of concern and pet names. Georgina's true deep feelings were a mystery to Mirembe. The one time she had seen her cry and show her emotions openly had been when her husband died.

She looked at her Mam's closed eyelids and wondered how it was possible to love someone so much when that someone was unable to express deep feelings.

Her soul was - is - beautiful, Mirembe thought. *She loved deeply but brought it matter-of-factly. She is - was - in fact the prototype of a matriarch, strong, no-nonsense, real, someone to vest my life upon. If only I can be half of what she was, I will be a good person.*

Chapter 10

FOR THE FIRST TIME in her life Mirembe grieved deeply and she had no idea how to do so. She had many Skype calls with Tessa, who pulled her through as best as she could, but the year after Georgina died was the lowest year of Mirembe's life.

Not only did she miss her Mam, but she was also at a loss as to what she wanted to do with her life and, as she was reaching thirty, she wondered if she would ever meet a man with whom she could have a family.

After the debacle with Martin DeBecker, there were few other men. She went out with a couple of young medical students a number of times, but it never led to anything, which now made Mirembe think she was not really relationship material.

Next to that, running the Atura household and the Lake Victoria estate proved more complicated than she had thought. Master Kevin grew grumpier by the day and Mirembe's professional eye detected the first signs of dementia. Michelle was a handful and she needed to get the girl an abortion and bail her out of jail. She had promised Georgina she would not fire the girl, but if that promise had not existed she would have kicked her out the same day.

Then there were the complicated accountant's visits that bored her stiff. She had to sit through them although she wondered why. To satisfy Mr Alexander's passion for numbers? He seemed in excellent control of everything, so had no need for her. And to top off her misery, Kitty developed a tumour as a result of which she had to put the poor dog down.

There were days when Mirembe dreamt of letting it all go, to escape to New York or Hong Kong and set up a practice in a new place and forget all about Africa, but her deep-rooted loyalty to her adopted parents kept her tied to Atura and Uganda.

Of her biological family she heard nothing and expected them to be living the same lives they had always lived. She could have asked Michelle, who went there on her red scooter every Saturday, but did not. She spoke to the girl as little as possible and did not want the wench to know she was longing for some sort of belonging, whatever it was.

That this was the passage of bereavement she endured, which made her feel so low and everything in her life so complicated, did not cross Mirembe's mind, despite Tessa telling her this every time. Experiencing an as yet unknown feeling, even Mirembe, highly educated in the material, failed to classify it from within.

WHEN A YEAR PASSED and poor Master Kevin had to be institutionalised because he kept forgetting to turn off the gas and wandered through the streets of Atura in his pyjamas, and Michelle chose to marry her boyfriend, a cousin of hers from the village, Mirembe decided it was time to close the shutters of the house in Atura and go on a long vacation.

That was what Mam had taught her was the best medicine against grief.

After backpacking in Thailand for three months, Mirembe got bored again and still did not know what to do except miss her Mam. She decided that enough was enough and a change was necessary. The simplicity of life as a backpacker and the nagging feeling that she still had to work through stuff in herself where her childhood was concerned, made her reach a radical decision.

She would return to the village and live in a hut by herself and try to grow closer to her biological mother and her brothers while it was still possible. Mirembe was sure that her discontent and depression was linked to that early childhood and she could only become a good child psychiatrist if she first healed herself.

MIREMBE MADE MINIMAL preparations for her return to the hamlet and consciously did not think too much ahead about what she would encounter. She understood people would look at her with strange eyes, so much was sure, and talk behind her back and think she was cooking up some investment plan because she was rich.

The main thing she desired was to live a simple life, without the luxury she was used to, and to find out what it would do to her, if it would bring her closer to her blood relatives, closer to herself, and silence the nagging negativity that ruined her days.

Next to that she would read all the novels she had always wanted to read, but had no time for during her medical training. The Kindle that had just been introduced would be a great help, because she would not have to carry a whole library with her and, as she had to visit Master Kevin in the home twice a week to play board games with him and take him for a walk, she had access to electricity to upload to her devices.

Those were the only luxuries she permitted herself; her phone, her laptop and her e-reader for as long as they were charged.

Finding a hut the villagers would allow her to stay in was the first hurdle; her mother - now in her early fifties, but still vigorous and loud-mouthed - was dead set against her daughter returning to the community.

This time her mother did not win. Chieftain Oidu called everyone together for a vote. Only Lwango and her sons voted against, all the others - purely out of curiosity - voted in favour.

"Well, if it must be," Lwango moaned, "let her come, but remember I called her Trouble is Born because trouble is what she is." But, being opportunistic too, she added, "Well, none of you folks can say you have a daughter who is rich and has a degree but still wants to live in a stinking hut. I think I'll ask her for the keys to her house in Atura. Ha ha."

However, Lwango's influence in the community was long in waning, especially after she started a relationship with a married man of the next village. Adultery was not accepted in the tribe and as a result she and her man had been generally ostracised.

To some extent this was a favourable situation for Mirembe.

HER ARRIVAL WAS LOOKED upon more with anticipation and curiosity than with resentment. Lots of goodwill came her way when she finally occupied the empty hut next to Oidu and his wife Nasiche, who had been present at her birth and secretly had always longed to take the little girl into her care when the mother acted so cold and heartless towards her.

Even if Mirembe desired inwardly to be alone, Nasiche kept inviting her to have dinner with her and her husband so she would not have to cook herself. As a result of all the invitations that followed, Mirembe hardly got time to read.

There was always a neighbour or a child seeking her attention. The children wanted to play on her phone or laptop and the adults came in for a chat. Women came to sweep her hut and little boys fought with each other to carry Miss Mirembe's water for her. A garden was created, and jewellery laid out in front of her hut for her to choose from.

At times it embarrassed her, and she consulted with the Chieftain how to deal with the people's curiosity but also generosity.

"Don't worry, Mirembe," he said, taking a long draw from his clay pipe. "You give the people a mission in life. Don't you see? They've never had anyone to look up to and now see how enraptured they are to be of help to you. The mere fact you've decided to return to your birthplace will make them do anything for you. And you give so much in return. You don't even realise that."

Mirembe stared out over the river and the sun sinking below it and had to admit the old man was right. It did feel like give and take. Only yesterday one of the women found out she was a doctor and immediately a line had formed in front of her hut with villagers asking for a cure for this ailment or that. She sighed happily. She finally felt useful again and, contradictory as it seemed, this simple community could essentially be the place where her sad heart would heal.

Even her own mother had asked her advice about a corn in her right foot that bothered her.

To all the requests, she had simply answered that next time she was in Akura she would pass by the local hospital and ask for an emergency medical kit.

IN THE WEEKS that followed, Mirembe lacked very little and, despite the rudimentary lifestyle she now adopted, she was happy as she had not been for a long time.

On a clear Saturday morning she was washing her spare dress and some other articles in the river, enjoying the splashing water and the clear voices of two naked little boys chasing each other nearby.

She was singing one of the children's hymns in her clear soprano while rinsing the soap from her clothes.

As she looked up, she was surprised to see a tall black man in the government's army uniform approach along the river bank carrying a backpack in the same camouflage print as his clothes and wearing the green beret with the Ugandan flag.

Although Mirmembe had always known of the on-going conflict with Kony and the LRA in the Northern provinces, they were over a hundred miles away from the hotbed of the Acoli district, so soldiers rarely showed themselves on the streets of Atura, let alone in the small unimportant hamlet on the river that did not even have a name.

Startled, but also curious, Mirembe observed her surroundings. No one seemed alarmed by the arrival of a soldier. The two boys kept splashing around in the water and the women kept chatting to each other while hanging up the washing.

On passing her, the soldier greeted her with a friendly smile and she was instantly knocked over by how handsome and strong he looked. This was a man who was confident and dedicated, army clothes or not. She could not help glancing around to see where he was headed and was astonished when he went straight for Oidu and Nasiche's hut.

Soon loud shrieks of happiness were heard.

Nasciche came running out of the hut crying out merrily, "Kaikara is home! Aren't we blessed?"

At that moment Mirembe understood the soldier had to be their eldest son, the one born the year before her, once her brother Mukisa's best friend. She banished pleasant thoughts about him from her mind as she walked back to her own hut and sat on her haunches to prepare her simple dinner of rice and vegetables.

Although she had been back in the community for five weeks now, none of her brothers or their wives had approached her, despite all the love and respect Mirmebe received from those outside her family. So, this Kaikara being friends with her family could not mean anything good.

The huts stood in such close proximity to each other, it was impossible not to overhear the conversation going on between Oidu and his son and, against her will, Mirembe listened in.

"When will this madness finally end, son?" the old man asked. "How long has Kony been pestering this country and our neighbouring countries? Almost twenty! How come the government army doesn't succeed in eradicating these criminals?"

"Ah, father," the younger man replied, "I cannot answer that question, but he and his main chiefs are as sly and slippery as eels. But you seem to forget that Operation Lightning Thunder was a success to some extent. He's no longer in the country and his influence is greatly diminished."

"That may well be," the father contradicted, "but the man is one of the greatest criminals this country has ever known, and he should be put behind bars."

"You seem to overlook what Idi Amin did to the country, father," Kaikara replied subtly, "but coming back to our situation in 2009, I can tell you that in all the seven years I've now been in the army, it is true we have gained little territory despite the help from the U.N. I will keep trying, father. That's all I can promise."

"Is it true he's hiding in the Democratic Republic of the Congo now, probably fathering more children there all the while reciting the Ten Commandments? Ha!" the father spit out angrily. "I wish I was twenty years younger and I'd smoke out the bastard myself!"

"Well, then I'm glad you aren't," Kaikara answered with a laugh. "I would not want you to be involved in such a horrible guerrilla fight, dear father. Kony may have left Ugandan soil and is hiding with our neighbours for fear of being sent to the International Court in The Hague and the army is only frying the small fish, but at least we've managed to free a couple of towns and villages from their terror in the Garamba region. The most important victory was setting free three hundred child soldiers held hostage in a school building for training purposes, but alas," and here the young man sighed deeply, "we've lost ten of our good men as well. Among them Peter Ocan from Atura, you know, the school master's son. It was an ambush, nothing we could do."

"Yes, I've heard." Oidu sighed as well. "Your mother and I went over to offer our condolences. Oh, son, I am always so glad you've returned safely, because I'm so afraid one day you will also not come back alive. You know I support your cause wholeheartedly and I also believe that the young men of Uganda should fight this monster, but my father's heart hurts on a daily basis. Not to talk of your mother who is developing a heart condition."

"I will visit the Ocans myself while on leave," Kaikara replied, "and I promise you I will do all that is in my power to always come back to you and Mother."

"Let's not talk of the war and fighting, son. Let me tell you the good news! We've actually got a doctor in our midst now. When your mother was complaining of the pains in her heart I sent her to

Mirembe - that's how the doctor is called - and she promised she will get her some proper medicine from the hospital, free of charge because we cannot afford these expensive pills."

"Mirembe?" she heard the soldier ask. "Isn't that the girl that was adopted by the Mayor and his wife years ago? What is she doing here?"

Mirembe felt her cheeks redden, but she had no idea why. Suddenly she had become the topic of their conversation and, knowing Oidu like the back of her hand, she was sure she would remain that topic for the rest of their conversation. Wondering whether she should leave her cooking and go for a walk so as to avoid further embarrassment, she made preparations to cover the chopped vegetables and get up, when she heard Oidu's shout.

"Mirembe, come over here, meet my son Kaikara! He's on leave from the army."

Now she had no escape and, cleaning her hands on her apron, reluctantly followed the chieftain's orders.

When she entered the neighbours' hut, the tall soldier had taken off his beret, showing short black hair and a strong rectangular face, very much like his father. He sat cross-legged on a mat sipping from a glass of mango tea, but got up to greet her, realising of course she was the woman he had seen at the river. He was so tall that he bumped his bed against the ceiling.

They both laughed, and he showed a row of teeth so clean and beautiful she could hardly take her eyes off them. They shook hands, while the father rubbed his hands contently.

"Sit with us, Mirembe. I guess Nasiche will return soon when she has boasted enough to all the other women that her strong son is back."

A silence fell, a slight tension hung in the air and Mirembe, with all her knowledge of human behaviour, felt tongue-tied and blank-minded.

Kaikara came to her rescue. "My father told me you are a doctor?"

She nodded and then thought he might think she still could not talk, so she quickly added, "Well, actually a psychiatrist, but for that you first have to become a medical doctor."

"I know," he laughed. "I may be a simple soldier, but I do know what study is required to become a psychiatrist."

Oidu kept nodding, continuing to sing her praises. "Mirembe is an angel incarnated, really she is, son. If you saw what changes she has already brought to the people here. Everyone loves Mirembe."

Again she blushed while Kaikara looked at her sideways and said, smiling warmly, "I can imagine that! Gosh, it's more than twenty years ago since you lived here. Of course, I knew you had become very beautiful, as we would all stare at you sitting in the front row in Church, but you've been away for a long time. And so have I," he added, looking more solemn.

"When did you become a soldier?" Mirembe asked, mostly to steer the conversation away from her looks.

"Ever since I was a little boy and we were taught about the civil war and Joseph Kony and his Lord's Resistance Army pestering our land, I have wanted to free my people from tyranny," he answered. "It's probably all schoolboy heroism, as I couldn't stop myself from reading about the American Civil War and realising a similar thing - of course under completely different circumstances - was happening to my own people. Then there was no stopping me, very much against the wishes of my parents who wanted me to be a good fisherman."

Again that laugh, again those beautiful teeth. Suddenly Mirembe knew the word; he was 'charismatic'.

Meanwhile Nasiche re-entered the hut and, seeing the two young people engaged in conversation, gave her husband a knowing wink and announced, "Mirembe, go and get your vegetables. You are going to have dinner with us tonight."

THAT NIGHT, LYING on her mat in her simple abode, Mirembe could not sleep. She was very aware of the tall young man lying only a couple of meters away from her and an immense longing came over her.

She wanted to be held by those strong arms, feel the roughness of that camouflage uniform, feel her lips against that beautiful mouth and sink deep into those kind, wise eyes. Despite their difference in standing and education, Mirembe was aware hers had only materialised because of good luck while Kaikara was educated in his own way. She was also sure he had no interest in her; why would anyone be interested in her? Plus, he probably had a girl in Kampala where he lived close to the military base. Maybe he was even married, but why would he not have brought his wife with him? Maybe she was with child or looking after their children and he would leave again tomorrow, only paying a fleeting visit to his old parents.

Thoughts kept racing through Mirembe's mind and at some point she got so sick and tired of herself that she wrapped herself in her Mam's quilt and, opening the flap of her hut, stepped into the silent darkness.

She sat down a little further along the river and inhaled the stillness of the night with gratitude, gazing at the millions of twinkling stars above her head and listening to the soft, soothing lapping of the water. Being outside immediately calmed her and made her thoughts more coherent.

What she felt for the uniformed man she had never felt before in her life and she now needed to analyse this new emotion, because one thing was crystal clear to her - she would never become the victim of another male again.

Her thoughts drifted to Tessa and how she and Paul had first laughed at this new undertaking of going back to basics, but, realising Mirembe was serious about her quest to find herself, they had supported her. They even promised to come and visit her next month, loyal friends as they were.

Then her thoughts floated to her adopted parents and to her biological father Oneka, whose graves she had tended that week. Mr Mayor and Mam and Dad all rested in the same corner of the Akura graveyard. Close together. How strange was that?

Sitting like this, letting her thoughts go, was blissful, so she was startled when she suddenly heard soft footsteps approaching her. Without turning her head, she knew who it was, and her heart leapt.

Could he be feeling the same, or was he again the player she should run from?

At the first words he spoke she knew the answer.

Chapter 11

"WOULD YOU LIKE ME to show you how to catch a fish, Doctor Kasozi?" Kaikara stood in the middle of a shallow part in the river, stripped to his waist, with a fishing rod in his hands, smiling broadly.

Mirembe lay on a mat under a parasol reading *War and Peace* on her Kindle while munching a piece of fleshy coconut. She looked up and as always was struck by his virile and muscled body and the ease with which he embodied his beauty and was not afraid to show it. Their friendship was growing fast, but no intimacies had taken place. They were both shy, both hurt and both uncertain how to go about it.

"Okay," Mirembe shouted back. "I don't think I'll be any good at it, but let me try."

Not caring that her dress would get wet - everything dried within minutes in the baking sun - she stuck her straw hat on her head and waded towards him. The water glistened, fish jumped above the surface a little further downstream and her heart beat fast every time she got close to him. Soon she would have to leave and get away from him, as the situation was becoming unbearable for her. She could not do anything without thinking about Kaikara, longing to be near him, talk with him, share experiences. Even *War and Peace*, a book she was actually rereading because she loved Tolstoy so much, could only hold her attention for a couple of minutes before it would return to her favourite subject - Kaikara and his godlike body.

Tomorrow I'll go to Atura and stay there until he's gone, she thought for the umpteenth time as she stood in front of him saying instead, "So what do I do?"

"Come here," he ordered. "I'll first show you how to throw. I'm really surprised your dad never taught you this. For sure he taught all your brothers." For a moment a shadow slid over Mirembe's happy face and Kaikara, sensitive as he was to her feelings, mumbled, "Sorry, shouldn't have said that."

"It's okay. It's the truth."

"Come here," he said again and, before she could do anything, she was caught in between the two magnificent bare arms holding a fishing rod. She was painfully aware of villagers staring at her and Kaikara murmuring softly in her hair," "Don't take any notice of them; I won't do anything inappropriate before their eyes."

Mirembe couldn't help giggling when he added loudly, "Now hold that rod still for a moment, Dr Kasozi, and concentrate," and then whispered so she could only hear, "For heaven's sake, Mirembe, I hope *you* can concentrate because I surely can't."

It was the first time he spoke her name and it was so sweet and loving that she indeed had great difficulty keeping herself together, but she eventually managed to throw the line out to land some thirty yards from her, where the brightly coloured float started bobbing on the water's surface.

"Nice throw, Doctor. Now catch the biggest fish in the river so we will all have dinner tonight," Kaikara shouted, all the while keeping her firmly in his embrace.

Actually, only through the power of his arms did Mirembe feel she was able to keep upright, as she was sure her legs would have given in under her if not for his support.

"Please release me," she whispered. "I feel so awkward with all of them staring at us. They will think we're a couple."

"I know," he whispered back understandingly, immediately releasing her from his grip. "I'd forgotten everything is put under a magnifying glass here in the village. In Kampala no one would care a dime if I held a girl or not."

Standing a little shakily, but soon finding her balance again, Mirembe was excited to see the float go down. "I've got one!"

"You sure have and it's a big one," Kaikara remarked. "Here, let me help you reel it in, before you lose it."

THAT NIGHT THEY decided to go to Mirembe's house in Atura to be away from the prying eyes of their relatives. Kaikara had only one week left before his leave was over and they wanted to make the most of it.

Now that the house was without servants, Mirembe found herself in a new situation, having to do everything herself in a place where she had never lifted a finger. Having lived in the village doing all the basic tasks that require survival, though, she could now heat the cooker and find her way among Master Kevin's pots and pans.

It was a blissful week, but also tinged with melancholy and strange demons from the past.

Kaikara lay in her bed - the very bed where she had been so frightened and alone when she arrived in the strange house as an eight year old - listening to Mirembe playing Vivaldi's *Four Seasons* on the Stradivarius her Mam bought her for her fifteenth birthday.

Vivaldi had been Mam's favourite composer and although Mirembe had not shared that passion at first, for love of her Mam she would always play Vivaldi. Now, she was overjoyed to hold the instrument again, which she had left behind with difficulty when going to the hut, afraid the damp nights might ruin the beautiful instrument, and it had also been a test.

Mirembe without her Stradivarius was not really Mirembe, but the violin had represented luxury and did not fit in the rudimentary lifestyle she sought. Back to basics had been the most important goal. She had literally stripped herself from everything, but now, having everything again, plus the love of a man, was almost too much for her tender heart.

Kaikara, strong as a horse and full of passion, was gentle and cautious with her, but she still felt vulnerable and had difficulty coping with the immense flood of emotions that suddenly washed over her.

Holding her instrument, she finally felt secure again and some of her former strength returned. When she put it back into its case, giving it a last gentle touch of love, she had no idea if she had been playing for fifteen minutes or for hours. Looking anxiously at Kaikara, she saw his eyes were full of tears and he beckoned her to come to him.

"What's wrong, dearest?" she asked, full of concern, slipping into his arms on the cover.

"Nkwagala nyo, I love you so much," he answered in Luganda as he took her body and wrapped it against his, shedding the warm tears on her bare shoulder. "Let me tell you why I'm crying. Five years ago, I was still a Private and it was only my second mission when we found ourselves in the outskirts of Gulu. I was really scared because the week before two of my friends, boys I'd done the military training with, had been killed in that area on a failed mission.

"I kept my fear at bay and used all my senses to find out where we were going without being attacked. There were eight in my group, creeping through the streets at night. I think it must have been around seven in the evening, pitch black, no moon. Two of my comrades had stayed in the jeep on the main road and we were supposed to find some of Kony's men in an old school building where they probably were holding people hostage.

"My eyes adjusted to the dark, because there were no streetlamps, and everything was eerily silent. A white cat with three legs suddenly lurched in front of me and disappeared in an overgrown garden. The suddenness of its presence momentarily freaked us out, but as one of my comrade's whispered 'good sign' we moved on. We had the school building in view and divided in two groups to encircle it. An extra battalion was on guard behind us. And that's when it happened.

"There was that sad, melodious sound of a string moving over the snares of a violin. It sounded out-of-world beautiful, but also spooky was that it was the only sound in the whole area. We did not know how to interpret it and stayed down, our guns directly pointing to the sound. There was no way we were going to shoot, but we were trained to direct guns at sounds."

He paused, wiping the tears from his face and kissing Mirembe's hair. "We didn't have to. There was just one shot and the violin fell silent. At that moment we besieged the building, entering it with full flashlight, ordering everyone to put down their weapons and surrender. Kony's men were taken by surprise and we killed all five of them. They were just children and one grown man. But what we found afterwards has marked me for life.

"When we had made sure there were no more enemies hiding in the building, we searched it and found ten terrified little girls huddled together in a corner. In front of them lay another little girl, bleeding profusely but with her violin still clamped in her little hand. We immediately tried to reanimate her, but she died in my arms."

Kaikara paused and in a coarse tear-filled voice continued, "Since the girl's senseless death, I've had difficulty listening to violin music. Also in this respect, dearest Mirembe, you are healing my heart."

They lay together in silence until dusk filled the room in a melancholy afterglow, both feeling what their mouths could not say in words. The bond between them was boundless, their divine fate sealed.

LATER, SITTING comfortably in the wooden rocking chairs on the veranda, biting into corn cobs while steaks sizzled on the barbeque, Mirembe found the courage to bring up their immediate future.

"You have to leave tomorrow. What then?"

Kaikara gave her his full attention, putting down his plate. "I know I don't want to think about it, but it is the reality. I have to go back to Kampala, to the barracks, and probably will be sent into South Sudan or Congo soon. What about you, us?"

Mirembe sighed. "I'll probably return to the village for a couple of weeks. My friends Tessa and Paul are visiting from Dublin and they will want to enjoy some simple time there, although I suppose we will probably mostly stay in Atura. To be honest, darling, I don't know. Before you came into my life, I was planning on taking a long time out, just to live the simple life until I really knew what I wanted to do. I was finding my feet there, you know; people started to depend on me and I saw all sorts of possibilities to modernise the com-munity without disrupting its original function of being a rural fishing community. But now?" She grabbed his hand and pressed it. "Now I'm so confused and so in love that I'd almost follow you into the war."

"You know, you would be of great use as a psychiatrist, sweetheart. There are masses of children traumatised by the incessant civil war. But you would need army training to be able to go with us."

"Let me think on it," Mirembe answered. "It has never entered my mind before and I shouldn't act on a whim. If I've learnt anything in these twenty-nine years then it's that. But right now please look at that meat. It's burning."

Smiling, Kaiakra got up and turned the steak. "Well, you decided overnight we would be a good pair together. Sometimes it's best to act on a whim."

Mirembe laughed. "I guess you're right, but going into a war is a totally different thing. Although my adopted father was a politician, being the mayor here, as you know, for some reason my parents have always kept the war and its reasons from me. It's only through you that I'm actually getting inside information about it. It doesn't seem like a good decision to simply adopt your mission in life as mine too."

Kaikara nodded, placing the golden steak with only a tiny black-burnt ridge on her plate. "Here's what I suggest then. I go back to the war because I have to, but because it is now fought outside Ugandan territory and it looks like Kony's influence is finally waning, I might be given another leave soon. You decide whether you want to continue your work in the village - it is not up to me to decide upon that - and in the meantime we'll text and phone and email each other so that during my next leave we'll have a plan. Idea?"

Mirembe agreed.

THEIR LAST NIGHT TOGETHER was bittersweet, their lovemaking slow and gentle as if afraid to break each other's heart, for that was how fragile they felt inside. Strong and healthy on the outside, their bodies craved passion, but the heart said 'gentle, I am in the pain of losing you'.

The fluidity and grace of their synchronic movements made their oneness feel like Elysium bliss wrapped in human frangibility, almost too much for the soul to take in. Heaven on earth was forever tinged with melancholy of the purest sort.

All the while through their moving as one, Mirembe wondered how it was possibly to care so much for someone in two weeks' and now shared Oidu and Nasiche's fear of losing him. He, who had captured her whole soul like a fisherman his fish.

Chapter 12

MIREMBE ADMIRED GEORGINA'S little dark fist with its cute little pink nails squeezing her index finger, while her daughter sucked at her mother's breast, almost falling asleep in the effort.

Nasiche, standing at the table folding a heap of pink baby clothes, remarked, "She's growing so fast, I bet Kaikara won't even recognise her when he comes home."

At that moment the door flung open and Nina, one of the nurses from Atura's new psychiatric wing, ran in. "Doctor, please come; Acanit is threatening to self-harm again unless you sit with her."

Although this alarming message was a vital disturbance in the rare moments of tranquillity Dr Mirembe Kasozi-Okello had in her busy life as medical director of Atura State Hospital, she instantly gave the infant to her mother-in-law and followed the young nurse to the ward.

"What's happened?" she asked, wriggling into her white coat that still did not fit properly as she had not lost her pregnancy pounds yet.

"She had a nightmare again, doctor. We tried to calm her ourselves as we didn't want to trouble you during your break, but somehow she's got hold of one of the knives from the kitchen. We really don't know how she managed that."

"Never mind, I'll see to her, Nina. Go back to your own work. Thank you," Mirembe said as she opened the door to a small bedroom with filtered light.

A girl of about twelve years old with big, frightened eyes sat in the corner of the room. Her skinny legs were tucked underneath her, and she had pulled her cotton dress over her protruding knees. She was far too small for her age, but her eyes already disclosed a lifetime of traumatic experiences. In her fist she clamped a large meat knife, which she raised defensively when Mirembe entered.

Acanit was one of thirty girls found in a deserted convent in the mountains on the South Sudan border, abused as sex slaves by the rebels, filthy and highly-traumatised. Her entire family had been killed by the resistance army, apart from one older brother who still had not been found, but was Acanit's only hope.

Mirembe sat on the girl's bed and simply waited. She did what she also did when she had to help people to the other side; focus, send prayers and messages through the air and sit still. When she felt the little girl relax a little, she shifted her position slightly so as to make her aware she was still with her.

Eventually the girl spoke. "Where were you, Doctor? I was asking for you, but the nurses said you wouldn't come today, so that's when I went to find the knife. I cannot bear it anymore."

Mirembe did not answer, and cautiously approached the girl, who gave her the knife without further objection. When she got hold of the sharp object, the doctor in her took over.

She said with authority, "Acanit, before we talk, I'm going to put this dangerous weapon outside, okay? We don't need it here when we talk."

The girl nodded and emerged from her corner, waiting for Mirembe while she placed the knife outside the door. As soon as she returned, the girl was in her arms, sobbing and whimpering like a hurt animal. Together they sat on the bed and for a long time Mirembe simply stroked the girl's hair and repeated the same words over and over, so they became a mantra for the bruised little soul.

"It's okay, my dear, you're safe now, nobody's going to harm you here, nobody, you hear me, nobody will harm my Acanit."

This would eventually calm the child, so she would be able to talk about her nightmare. It was

175

always the same. Two men held her down; one man raped her and then the other, repeatedly until she lost consciousness. It was not even a nightmare; for four months, 120 days, this had been Acanit's reality.

Sometimes, because the hell had lasted so long, she did not know if she was dreaming or if she was still in reality being raped. Mirembe had already attempted to untangle the girl's new memories from her past, but so far without much result. She knew Acanit hovered on the edge and might give in any day.

With all her capacity, she tried to save her life, but oftentimes worried she had come too late. If the girl had not been such a danger to herself and her surroundings, Mirembe would have loved to take her into her own house to allow the girl to heal by letting her help with Georgina, but she could not put her own family in jeopardy.

In moments such as these Mirembe prayed to her Lord Universe in angry, yet endearing words. "What has happened to the African soul? Look how men and women suffer, small children. What has become of human civilisation in the 21st Century, Lord Universe? How can I, small as I am, alleviate such suffering?"

WHEN, HOURS LATER, Acanit was asleep again, heavily sedated and secured in a protective one-piece overall that also held her arms, Mirembe sat on the veranda of her house thinking about all the suffering that went on in her hospital nearby. She knew now why she had chosen to become a child psychiatrist and how she was helping her people.

"One day," she said to herself, "I hope Acanit will be a proud African woman, ready to change the world. If it is anywhere in my power, I will bring that about."

Then her thoughts drifted to her husband Kaikara, still fighting in South Sudan against the reasons for victims like Acanit and, as always, she experienced a mixture of love and worry. He had promised to lay down his military career.

The conflict was no longer on Ugandan soil and he felt he had done his duty, but having been in the army for so long and trained only to fight, he had no idea what he wanted to do in civilian life and this bothered him.

No matter that Mirembe told him time and again that he could do so much good in the hospital, like her he did not wish for his professional life to be dependent on hers. But she longed for him to come home and, after the birth of their daughter three months earlier, the longing was even stronger. They needed to be a family now, living together under the same roof, but Kaikara had also uttered doubts about living in small town like Atura. He loved either the buzz of Kampala or the quietness of the huts on the riverside, but could not find his soul in a provincial town with nothing but a couple of shops.

"Our lives are never going to be normal or average anyway," he said. "I know you won't remain the managing doctor of a small hospital, Mirembe dear. You're too clever for that. So why not move to Kampala straight away and open a clinic there?"

Taking over the small hospital in Atura had not been Mirembe's plan at first, but when the old manager, Dr Robert, died and people were out of sorts because they were afraid they would be deprived of medical help, Mirembe chose to jump in. And, because she was now the wife of Colonel Okello, the government decided to send war victims to her hospital and pump money into it. It would become an outstanding facility.

This meant she could not leave as easily anymore and Kaikara was well aware of that. From the very start of their relationship they had agreed they would not live as other couples did, instead giving each other space for their wishes and their careers. Therefore, if Kaikara found a job he wanted with the government in the capital, she was happy to go along with that, knowing well he would not be able to stay away from his wife and daughter for long.

Still, sitting in her rocking chair on her veranda, mulling over her life while her daughter slept peacefully and her patients were well fed and looked after, Mirembe wondered what it was she was missing.

Her husband of course, but was there something else? Yes, she was missing a female friend. Tessa, so far away, came vividly before her eyes, her bony, alabaster Celtic friend, with her big laugh and witty remarks, the friend she confided in, much like the relationship she had with her Mam. That feeling of female togetherness. Al-though she got on well with her mother-in-law, Nasiche remained simple and straightforward, not someone you could share your passions and your heart with.

"I am lonely," Mirembe acknowledged, "despite the fact I have everything I ever dreamt of, a husband, a child, a family, work that matters. I have no female friend near, that special bond almost as strong as a love relationship. Well, it is a love relationship. Women should bond together, that's what changes this world. But where can I find a friend in this little town? There is little chance I'll meet someone here. I would love to take Georgina to Dublin to see Tess and John, but I'm tied to the hospital. Maybe they can come for Christmas?"

SOON MIREMBE WAS too busy with her work and child to remember her ponderings, and the nagging loneliness vanished once again to the back of her mind. Kaikara came home and everything was bliss once more, and he decided for the time being to settle with wife and child in Atura and help out in the hospital.

And then the great breakthrough came for Acanit. She finally responded well to the therapy and anti-depressant medication. She could now go to school for the first time in her dark-blue uniform and white blouse, as proud as a peahen.

Mirembe took her to school herself and she swallowed her tears when she saw her protégé take her place in the row of school desks and take out her books. She knew how bright this girl was and

Africa's sun now poured down on her small head and shoulders, on which the next generations would stand.

Acanit moved in with them, and little Georgina, as yet unawares, moved up a little to make place for a big sister. Mirembe was pregnant again; this time it would be a boy who would proudly take his late grandpa's name - Henry.

Kaikara had grumbled that his family's names were not given a place for his children, but Mirembe had laughed and said, "Next time, dear!"

DURING THE FINAL months of Mirembe's pregnancy, a young doctor, Gabriel Otala, from Entebbe, was appointed to take over during her leave. As he was also training to become a psychiatrist, Mirembe felt her hospital was in good hands and she had some freedom to move around.

Soon after Henry was born, the family went travelling for a while, also to give Kaikara time to find out what he really wanted to do professionally.

He missed the army and the strong camaraderie that was an integral part of it and could not find his passion as the administrator and general supplies overseer of the hospital.

They were sitting in their rented New York apartment while the two young children were asleep, brainstorming about the future, when the phone rang. There was always going to be an unwanted intervention, no matter if they wished otherwise.

It was Nasiche. "Your dad is not well. I am so sorry to interrupt you, but I don't know how long he will last. Please never tell him I called you, for he forbade me to do so."

And thus Kaikara's future had to be pushed to the background again as they hopped on the next flight to Kampala.

ARRIVING AT THE HUT two days later, they found the old man dehydrated and hallucinating.

Kaikara was furious with his mother. "Why did you let this happen? Have you no thought in your brain?"

The poor woman defended herself by insisting Oidu had not wanted to leave the hut and go to hospital. "Mirembe, even your mother Lwango tried to persuade him on your behalf," Nasiche lamented.

This surprised Mirembe, but made her think somewhat more benevolent thoughts about her mother.

A new problem arose. Both Mirembe and Kaikara realised that with Oidu passing away, he as his eldest son would immediately be considered Chieftain of the community, which also included four other settlements down the river. Although it seemed an old-fashioned system in 2011, it was still held in high esteem and the villagers would be disappointed if he did not accept the honour. After all, it was his great-grandfather, also called Kaikara, who had founded the settlements.

"He may recover," Kaikara said hopefully, as he now regarded his future completely shattered by this sudden event, "or I could ask my brother to do it in my place. He's called after the old man, so seems to fit better, right?"

"We should have considered it before," Mirembe acknowledged. "How stupid that I never thought about it. We'll find a way out of it. Maybe you can do it part-time?"

"Let's concentrate on Father while he's still alive," Kaikara responded. "Is he strong enough to be transported to the hospital?"

Mirembe shook her head doubtfully. "But I'll ask Gabriel to bring the mobile hospital right away. It can be here in two hours."

And so they did. It was the first time the villagers saw the tent arrive at the hamlet, with the camp bed and all the equipment, and they peeked around the canvas walls, the small children even

185

lifting the material from the bottom to see what was going on inside.

Oidu lay on the stretcher with a drip in his arm, breathing shallowly. Mirembe's human heart wanted to save him, but her doctor's heart knew what she was trying to do was sheer madness. The Chieftain wanted to die and die he would, so she let her doctor's heart rest and began the transit with the wise old man. Oidu had a beautiful death and was laid to rest next to his friend, Mirembe's father, Oneka. They had been livelong friends and needed each other beyond the portals of death.

FOR SOME REASON the Chieftain's death affected Lwango and for the first time ever she sought closeness to her daughter. She was also kind to Nasiche, who had always defended her even when she got entangled with the married man and was ignored by the rest of the village.

Mirembe and her mother sat down for an awkward talk.

"How are the children?" her mother asked almost shyly.

"They are fine."

The word 'mother' would not pass Mirembe's lips, but she did not know which other word to use for her. Her Christian name? Ma'am? She decided to refrain from addressing her in any particular way.

"How old are they now?"

"Georgina will be three in October and Henry is four months."

Her biological mother winced at the names of her children and Mirembe realised she probably finally understood what she did to her daughter all those years ago.

But the old fox hadn't lost its tail yet. "Whom do you love more? The girl or the boy?"

"That's no question to ask me! I love them both equally and always will. I will make sure my daughter is not met with any resistance to become what she wants to become. Both she and her brother are unfortunately born in a culture where girls are by some still considered inferior."

187

She stressed the word 'inferior' and looked at her mother with fierceness in her eyes. Then she sighed; this simple woman who happened to be her biological mother was also a product of her upbringing and could not be held responsible for her beliefs. It was up to her, Mirembe, who had been given chances most girls in her area would never have, to change those beliefs.

She spontaneously added, "Shall I bring them next time for you to see?"

The look on Lwango's face spoke volumes. "Would you? That would make me the happiest grandmother on this earth."

With this promise the two women parted, Lwango all happy and content and Mirembe wondering what would have happened to her had she been brought up by this woman.

As many times before, she felt eternally grateful to her adoptive parents.

Chapter 13

AFTER MUCH DELIBERATION among the elders of the settlements on the river, it was decided that Kaikara and his family would spend the summer months in the hamlet, where they constructed a slightly more luxurious hut than the simple abodes in which the rest of the families still lived. The rest of the year their Chieftain would be a high official at the Ministry of Defence in Kampala. It was also agreed that he would leave this position as leader of the community whenever he was needed in office or wanted to travel with his family.

Mirembe continued to be available for Atura hospital, but Gabriel was really in charge. She therefore set out, furthering what she started on her first return to the hamlet, to help modernise the community and get basic hygiene in place. Acanit was following in her footsteps and was now at boarding school in the capital, which gave her more time in the hamlet.

During the months Kaikara worked in Kampala, she decided to follow up on her realisation that she needed a female friend and took the children to Dublin to spend time with Tessa and John.

As her apartment on the second floor was still available to her, she was glad to bivouac there for a while and feel the much needed presence of intelligent, warm friends who had nothing but her wellbeing in mind. Having never been blessed with children of their own, Tessa and John loved being auntie and uncle and this gave Mirembe time to visit her beloved Dublin again and meet up with friends from medical school who had stayed in the area.

Most of all she loved the long talks with Tessa, her twin sister in a totally different body and from a completely different background, but with the same heart and the same passion - healing wounded souls. They forgot time when talking about their ideas and plans, immersed in the warm bath of true friendship.

Kaikara decided to join them for a couple of weeks and was thrilled to see the city that had been so influential on his wife, but in late May they were forced to return. Kaikara had to be in the village and Mirembe decided she wanted some down time there as well.

After the summer little Georgina would to go to school and, for the time being, they decided to place her in the elementary school in Atura, which meant Mirembe needed to return there to be home for their daughter. Time out in the hamlet before that happened would be good for all of them.

GABRIEL HAD EMPLOYED a Dutch/South African couple, Angela and Giles Johnson, previously aid workers on the outskirts of Kampala who had found it too crowded there and looked for a smaller place to continue their work.

Mirembe had not met them yet and on her return to the community she heard Angela and her husband Giles had a two-year old son, Nathan, born during their stay in Kampala. He apparently suffered severe ear infections for which they had temporarily returned to their home town in the Netherlands for proper treatment.

However, in the humid climate of the low countries, the little boy developed bronchitis, and they eventually came back to Uganda, hoping that the warm African sun would help him more.

He was seemingly a fragile child and a great source of worry for his parents. Being close to the hospital in Atura, they were in fact in the best place. Mirembe always made sure the hospital had the latest equipment.

For the time being, though, Mirembe was too involved with settling into their simple hut life again after cosmopolitan Dublin. She still enjoyed the simplicity of the lifestyle, and it always reminded her of how she had found there the love of her life. There were more reasons now, of course, such as the growing understanding between her and her mother, and teaching her children to remain connected to their nomadic roots and how to survive in basic conditions.

While, in his role as new Chieftain, Kaikara was consulted daily about domestic problems and small arguments or the distribution of land and property, the simple life was blissful.

Therefore, when it reached Mirembe's ears that the little boy Nathan had died, she was shocked and, leaving her two kids in the care of Nasiche and her husband, she set out for Atura immediately.

GABRIEL HAD TOLD HER that the Johnsons rented a house in the same street where Mirembe's house also stood, next door in fact, so when she arrived she knew where to go.

She saw Angela sitting on the veranda, looking forlorn, frozen, with her arms clasped around her pulled-up knees. Giles was not with her.

Mirembe approached her carefully, knowing the Dutch woman would probably not appreciate her company, but being sure the family had no relatives around yet, she felt it her obligation to sit with her. She also felt slightly guilty she had not visited the young family before and looked into the little boy's medical record to see if she could have been of help.

It was seldom foreigners showed interest in this remote part of Uganda and for that reason alone they should be given a warm welcome, having left their safe and wealthy country behind to help out others in need. Mirembe did not know what their qualifications were, but as they had been in Uganda consistently over the past few years, the couple had to like it and probably spoke some Luganda.

Angela did not seem to see her, so Mirembe sat on the steps of the porch to let the grieving woman, blond and blue-eyed like many people from the countries high above the equator, get used to her presence. Not able to see her face, as Mirembe sat with her back to her, she heard the woman get up from her seat as she had anticipated, but she quietly remained where she was, her hands folded in her lap, gazing at the red sun sinking over the river.

As always, Mirembe sent prayers out to the dead on yonder side and to the bereaved on this side, asking her Lord Universe to strengthen the grieving woman and her equally grieving husband.

She heard the woman sit down again and gave an inaudible sigh of relief. It meant Angela had accepted her presence. This was the first step; now it was a matter of concentrating on the foreign energy Mirembe was unacquainted with and, as she also never had seen the little boy now dead, she had to form a picture of him in her mind before laying his body symbolically back on his mother's lap to comfort her.

His little spirit was still fighting the death that had overcome him as he had been fighting for all the days of his short two year life, and Mirembe had difficulty making him understand and accept he was dead and to return his spirit to his parents.

But, finally, she managed to make him understand and then sensed Angela relax a little.

Meanwhile it grew dark and chilly. The streets of Atura were deserted, but at some point she heard a car approaching. It stopped in front of the house and a tall dishevelled man got out. Mirembe moved out of his way, so he could race up the steps of the porch to be with his wife.

"I'm so sorry, darling, to have taken so long! Agony, pure agony!"

Now the husband was home, Mirembe felt she no longer needed to sit with the woman and started to walk to her own house, desiring a hot cup of tea and a cheese sandwich.

Angela called out to her, "Dear lady, I'm so sorry, I haven't talked to you. You see, I'm all upset."

"I know," Mirembe replied kindly, "that's why I came to sit with you. My sincere condolences to you both."

Tears started to pour down the poor mother's cheeks and her husband quickly put his arm around her, fighting his own tears.

"I'll come back tomorrow if you want? I live next door, you see."

At that moment Angela opened her eyes wide and exclaimed, "Oh, my goodness, you must be Doctor Kasozi, I had no idea. Oh, please, do come in!" She opened the screen door to their living room with an inviting gesture.

"Are you sure?" Mirembe asked.

"Of course, we've wanted to talk to you since we arrived here, but Gabriel told us you were in Dublin."

"I was for a while, but I've been back in my rural community since last week. Please, let us not talk of me. I'm here to help you, that is, if I can be of any help in this unfortunate situation."

"Thank you for just being here," Giles said. "Let's ask Simone to make us some tea. I think we can all do with some tea."

"Where is your little boy, if I may ask?" Mirembe asked.

"He's in the hospital morgue right now," Giles said. "The authorities wouldn't let me take him home. Gabriel tried with all his might, but the municipality was unrelenting. Too hot to take to a private home they said."

The poor man ground his teeth and Mirembe was instantly on her feet again.

"Let me try," she said. "You two have your tea. You need it more than I do. I'll be back as quickly as I can."

Still acquainted with most of the officials from the time her adopted dad was the mayor of Atura, Mirembe set out to the house of the current mayor first.

The job was done in no time and she asked the undertaker to bring a cooling system to the grieving parents' house as well when he delivered the little boy's body. Then she requested two nurses from the hospital to come and lay the boy out. She ordered candles, flowers and prayer books; all was done within the hour. Not knowing whether the Johnsons were religious, she contacted the priest, but told him to wait in the wings.

Then she returned to the couple's house and accepted that much needed cup of tea.

MIREMBE ENDED UP arranging everything for Nathan's funeral. The parents could not think coherently and were also unfamiliar with African procedures. They did know they still wanted to work as aid workers for the Red Cross in Uganda for at least another couple of years, and decided to have their son buried in the Atura cemetery, so he would be close by. For the rest, they were so caught up in their bereavement that they hardly paid attention to the details and let Mirembe organise it for them.

It was the saddest funeral she had ever arranged, but due to those nagging guilty feelings that kept creeping up on her, she was glad she could be of help. Despite the fact that Angela and Giles told her many times she was not to blame for Nathan's death, that she probably would have been unable to find a cure for him also, as the meningitis was diagnosed too late and the antibiotics failed to work, that the little boy was delicate from birth and Gabriel did everything he could, something told Mirembe she would have diagnosed meningitis from its inception and it would not have been too late.

They would never know now.

AS SHE FELT RESPONSIBLE for the couple sobbing their hearts out one moment and in apathetic silence the next, she decided they needed her more than the people in her village. She would stay in their neighbourhood until their respective families arrived from Holland and South Africa.

Not knowing how long this was going to take, she brought her children to her home in Atura, because she too needed them with her at this difficult time, while aware that her two healthy children might prove difficult for Angela and Giles. She asked Nasiche, who had come to look after them, to keep them out of sight.

At some point, though, Angela heard their little voices behind the fence that separated their gardens.

"Are these your children, Mirembe?" Angela asked, and she nodded, not knowing what to say.

"How old are they?"

"Four and one. A girl and a boy."

Angela sighed. She appeared almost translucent in her grief, with dark patches under her eyes, her shoulders hanging and her eyes filling with tears suddenly and randomly.

Chewing her lips and eyeing her own dead boy in a small white open coffin in the back room, hidden under a mosquito net against the flies and surrounded by the constant buzzing of the cooling machine underneath him, she mumbled through her tears, "Can I see them?"

"Are you sure you want to?" Mirembe asked, with a concerned look at the ghostlike mother. "Just not here."

"No, outside, on the veranda. I won't leave my boy, you know." Angela spoke the words quickly.

"I'll fetch them then."

Five minutes later she arrived with Georgina at her hand and little Henry on her arm. Moving cautiously towards Angela, who stood unmoving on the veranda, her hands clasped around the railing, knuckles white from her effort to keep herself together, Mirembe suddenly thought she was grateful her children where black, as that at least would not remind Angela of the white little angel lying in his coffin.

Georgina, who had inherited her mother's sensitivity when it came to other people's feelings, tugged on her mother's hand, wailing, "Please, mummy, I want to go back to Grandma Nas."

"We're just going to say hello to our neighbour, Georgie. That's only polite."

"She doesn't look happy, Mammy," the little girl tried again.

Her brother, contented on his mother's arm, nestled closer to her and, taking out his thumb, eyed the white woman staring at him with big eyes. To avoid the intent stare of the stranger, he turned his head and laid it on his mother's shoulder.

When they were moving up the stairs of the porch, a change came over little Georgina and she went straight into the strange woman's arms, crying with big gulps. Angela looked at Mirembe helplessly over the child's head, but instinctively threw her arms around the sobbing girl.

"She knows your pain," Mirembe uttered. "Just let her. It will comfort you as well."

Angela caressed the wiry curls in tiny braids that felt so different from Nathan's silky hair. Then Georgina insisted on sitting on Angela's lap in the wooden rocking chair. Mirembe noticed how her daughter's warm, round body was a comfort to the mother, who's entire being struggled with the intense loss she experienced.

That evening Angela's parents were due to arrive with her younger sister, and also Giles' father and grandfather. His mother was unable to come as she had to stay with his invalid brother. The funeral was scheduled for the next morning.

"Will you and your husband please be present at the funeral?" Angela asked. "You've arranged almost everything, so it would be really strange if you weren't. Plus, I'd like you to meet our families."

"Only if you and Giles want that. Kaikara is supposed to come tonight anyway, so I can ask him."

Georgina pricked up her ears. "Is Daddy coming? Then you can meet my daddy, Auntie."

Both women smiled at the girl's instant liking of Angela. It was a blessing under the circumstances.

"Come, Georgie, we have to leave Auntie alone now. She has things to do."

At that the little girl turned her round face to Angela and whispered, "Can I see him, Auntie?"

Angela sent a puzzled glance at Mirembe, who was also surprised, but instantly remembered herself at that age, feeling and knowing everything.

"Shall I let her?" Angela asked.

"If she wants to, she can handle it," the mother replied, "but I'm not taking Henry in, so it must be the two of you."

Chapter 14

AFTER THE FUNERAL, the Johnsons, needing temporary absence from the gaping wound of losing their son, went back with Angela's parents to Holland to recover, but a week later Angela phoned.

"Mirembe, I can't stand it here anymore. I'm feeling so depressed. I need your presence, your wisdom. Don't get me wrong, people are nice here and it's great to be home, but I feel like I'm suffocating. No one mentions Nathan, and everyone acts as if he never existed. Even my own parents just try to be cheerful all the time and want me to go outside to get fresh air when all I want is to lie in bed and cry and sleep.

"Giles is not much help either; he's turned into an oyster. We can't talk anymore, certainly not about Nathan. What am I to do? Of course, you cannot come here; you have your own family. Maybe I should return to Uganda and be with you? I feel like you understand me a lot better than my own family. Oh, what should I do?"

She kept talking and talking and Mirembe just listened.

No matter if she wanted to go to Holland, it was impossible at this time. Henry was teething and being a nuisance, and Georgina was settling in her school and needed her as well. Next to that, Gabriel was finally finishing his PhD in Entebbe, so the hospital was again Mirembe's responsibility.

"Listen, Angela, from my experience as a psychiatrist I would suggest you try it a few more days with your parents, but if you truly feel you're getting worse because they can't give you the attention you need, then return to Uganda. I think you might have become more African in the years you lived here, and our way of life goes much further than skin-deep. We know better how to mourn and how to help people through that first period, because we accept death is part of life. We let grieving people be, whether raging or silent, we don't condemn, don't silence them and don't silence the deceased."

After Angela hung up, sounding a little less depressed, Mirembe sat down and thought about their conversation. As she had only been exposed to her own culture when it came to death and grieving, she had never considered that in other cultures people might be unable to show their grief after a loved one died.

Now she remembered that Tessa told her, when her mother died - Tessa had been eight years old - the Catholic priest, mighty and terrifying in his long chasuble, came thundering into their house late at night and the day after her mother was buried, and no one ever talked about her again. As they were five children, with Tessa the middle one, her father remarried within a year and that was all there was to her mother's memory.

Only during her psychiatric studies did Tessa realise she carried a huge hole in herself, which until then had never surfaced or properly healed. She visited her mother's grave, after finding out from an aunt where she was buried, and was devastated to find it overgrown with weeds and without even a proper headstone. Tessa had not blamed her father, who was working extra shifts in the milling industry to feed their mouths and at least - different from many of her schoolmates' fathers - did not spend his wages in the pub.

Combining Tessa's experience with what Angela was expressing now, Mirembe thought about bereavement in different cultures and soon she was browsing the internet reading all there was about the subject.

She was shocked by the number of grieving parents in western society ending up in institutions or heavily medicated because the death of their children was a topic either avoided or ignored. Self-help groups seemed the only option, as bereavement therapies proved mostly ineffective, but in the untrained self-help groups drop-out rates were high.

Mirembe was fired up to research a neglected topic related to her profession and could not stop reading and researching. What to her had come so naturally, even when a child - to sit with dying people and help the families afterwards - was partly ingrained in her culture, but also partly who she was. She knew in some African countries loud lamentations and ceremony accompanied bereavement, but she herself had never been an advocate of that. It depended on the wish of the family, of course.

"Time to talk to Kaikara," she remarked to herself, closing her laptop.

She had no concrete idea yet, but a study was presenting itself to her. It seemed as if the path she had been set on as a young girl now finally culminated in a profession - to help people with death and bereavement. It seemed so simple to her; not the process itself, but the help people required.

"Wait for Angela to return and find her feet again," Kaikara advised, after listening to his wife with a deep frown on his forehead, showing he was giving her all his attention. "I definitely think you're on to something, but you will need her to give you more information on how she is experiencing this period and she needs to be able to stand aside enough from her own process to express herself to you."

"Not necessarily so," Mirembe contradicted. "The fact she is actually going through it now could give me first-hand information on what it is lacking and how bereavement should be approached to feel more heard and understood."

"And are you so sure we have the right answers in our culture when it comes to mourning rituals?" Kaikara asked.

This question made Mirembe realise how much her husband was growing in his role of Chieftain. He always had the wisdom, but now he needed to show it and make it work for his people.

211

"It is a mixture of cultural behaviour and my own beliefs," Mirembe said. "Since early childhood I have done this intuitively and knew it helped people, both the deceased and the bereaved, but I had no idea how I did it. Even after becoming a psychiatrist, I have never considered sitting with the dying and comforting the bereaved a professional thing, only a human thing. Now I'm ready to study what it is I'm actually doing and to describe it so other people can learn it too. I do believe a large part of it is hypnosis, or meditation, or prayer, or whatever you would call slowing down brain waves.

"And this is, of course, tricky stuff to describe from a medical standpoint and get it published in a scientific journal, but I couldn't care less. I'm not on a mission to have the Board of Psychiatrists on my side. What I want is practical help, so that people wherever they are learn to accept death as a part of life and that, as a result, mourning their loved ones should have its proper place, and afterwards they will be able to build a new life for themselves and not remain crippled by unhealed wounds. How can they celebrate the life of their deceased loved ones and set them truly free, if they keep dragging them along in despair? The dead need their freedom, as you know."

"Yes, wife," Kaikara agreed, "but it's the most difficult thing to ask of the living. I think people in the West will continue to hang on to their dead as they do to their possessions. Having and owning is so much part of their culture that letting go are words they might like to profess with their lips, but find impossible to live by."

"I will give it some time to stew," Mirembe said thoughtfully, "but you do agree with me that this is my mission?"

"I don't have a single doubt on God's green Earth that it is," her husband said, kissing her tenderly. "You're a visionary and a saint, my dear. But can I have a kiss now, as I'm just a simple Chieftain in need of a kiss?"

Chapter 15

"WHAT KIND OF ATTENTION would you have wanted most in the first period of bereavement?" Mirembe looked up from typing on her laptop at the elderly couple sitting across from her, realising she was exhausted.

This was the twentieth interview today, and it had been like this for the past three weeks, collecting data from bereaved parents in her rented apartment on the Prinsengracht in Amsterdam, probably a stone's throw away from where that awful Martin DeBecker conducted his businesses. She involuntarily shivered thinking of him.

Everything was different and unusual in this country, most of all the people. On the outside they seemed quite happy, carefree and tolerant, but they were remarkably standoffish and closed-off where their feelings were concerned, very good at labelling and critiquing others, but lost in the maze of emotions and how to express them, especially when under great strain due to unexpected grief.

Although Angela warned her about her culture, this almost nonchalant skipping over deep feelings was what had surprised Mirembe most during her interviews.

Get on with living, the past is the past, no one will listen to me anyway, I have to give it a place, life's a bitch, time will heal the wounds.

It had been two years since the Johnsons lost their little boy and, after the year-long therapy Angela needed to come to grips with her intense feelings of bereavement, the two women became great friends. Mirembe finally had that much-longed for female friend close by.

Initially, though - when contact was mainly therapeutic - Mirembe had worried about her ability to help Angela. She had not trained as a bereavement specialist, rather primarily as a child psychiatrist, but the grieving mother insisted Mirembe was the only one who could help her.

Angela had indeed recovered remarkably, still enduring periods of intense pain and emptiness, but accepting these emotions now instead of suppressing them. She had also learnt not to bring up the topic with people who could not cope with her grief, as they would only say stupid things, and had equally accepted that her marriage to Giles had not withstood the pressure of their loss. Giles returned to South-Africa and, though they remained on a friendly foot, contact had withered to almost non-existent.

At first Angela stayed in Holland and tried to work as a social worker with difficult youngsters in one of Rotterdam's impoverished districts, with high crime rates and substantial drug abuse. Not able to find her own balance due to the break-up of her marriage and the stone-walling of her grief, she returned to the Africa that was now in her heart and soul. And to Mirembe.

While Angela grew stronger and came to understand that bereavement was a passage of the soul, she also became an advocate of Mirembe's healing therapy based on warmth, presence and healing touch. She was the psychiatrist's biggest promoter and kept telling anyone who cared to hear it that Mirembe's approach would save many others from falling in the eternal death-trap of unhealed grief.

Also, in consultation with Tessa, the two psychiatrists set out to create the questionnaires to map the lack of proper help western people experienced during bereavement.

As Tessa held her interviews in Dublin and Mirembe in Holland, they met up and worked together towards the end results that would be published in various scientific journals.

Now it was time to write the report and test the therapy. The outcomes of the interviews showed great overlap and made drawing conclusions simple and straightforward.

All the bereaved claimed they felt misunderstood and left to a large extent to their own devices soon after their loved one had died. They had no preparation for bereavement, as it had never been talked about by their families or taught in school. As they often did not know what they needed, swinging from wanting to be left alone to craving company, the incoherent messages they signalled to others sent most well-wishers flying away at the first signs of wanting to be left alone with their grief.

When asked what they needed most, it was someone being there, not talking to them, just their presence, so that if they wanted to talk, they knew they would not be talking to the walls.

Next up was the need for a hug, physical proximity, a shoulder to cry on. In third place came words, verbal exchange, as the bereaved often felt the words people spoke to them did not have the correct tonality for their sensitive beings. Even though people tried to say the right things, it never felt that way.

Words could also create distance, whereas presence and physical warmth always felt pure and therefore easier to accept.

Many who had tried to talk to a professional found these people unequipped, uttering platitudes such as, *it will get less painful* and *you have to give it time*. Professionals even interfered with their own bereavement stories. Open attentive listening was what most people said lacked, whether these were laymen or professionals.

Self-help groups seemed the best option. At least there were shared experiences and folk knew better what worked and what did not. The only problem with these groups was that some people sucked up everyone's attention. Many also found the different ways in which other bereaved coped with their loss irritating or useless. Some hated wailing, or incessant victimising; others hated people going back to work the next week and conducting business as usual.

MIREMBE WAS GLAD when the last interview was done and she had some time to herself. Later that evening Angela would join her, and they would go out for dinner together, but now she needed a long bath and face-time with her kids.

Acanit had sent her a WhatsApp - *Mam, if you have time, please call me!* - and, smiling to herself while throwing articles of clothing one by one on the floor and stepping into her hot bath, she dialled her foster daughter's number.

Acanit was a real lady now, eleven years old and preparing herself for secondary school, very good at maths and physics and lately dreaming of becoming a famous astronomer.

"Hi, sweetheart," she said, realising how much she was starting to sound like her own Mam, "how's my big girl?"

"I'm fine, Mam," Acanit's high choice rang in her ears. "I've got big news! My brother Mugisha has been found. He's been released from the LRA. Isn't that fantastic news?"

"It is, my dearest," Mirembe answered, while instantly wondering in what condition the child soldier had been found and how traumatised or brainwashed he would be. "That's the best news we've had in years. So where is he now?"

"I don't know, Mam. Dad called me to tell me that he had been told in the office and he's finding out where Mugisha is and has promised to go and bring him to Kampala as soon as possible. When will you be back, Mam?"

"I'm coming home this weekend, dearest. I need to be there when your brother arrives. You do understand he might be in a poor state?"

"I do, Mam, that's why I want you and Dad to be there, so you can help him. Do you think he might not know me anymore? Sometimes I'm afraid I won't be able to recognise him. It's been four years, you see. He was only eight when he was taken."

"Don't think too far ahead, Acanit. We will deal with it as it comes. You know he will be part of the family, just as you are?"

"I know, Mam. I have to go. I still have to do my homework."

"Will you be okay, my child? I'm sorry I am so far away from you right now. It must bring all sorts of nasty memories back to you, too." Mirembe knew the fragility of her adopted daughter.

"Really, I'm okay, Mam. Dad is in Kampala and he's promised to take me for a walk later on. Thank you, Mam."

Face-timing later with her two uncomplicated, happy children was a delight and soothed Mirembe's weary mind.

Maybe I'm taking on too much and travel too far from my children, she thought, *but I need to be an example to them. Staying in a hut at the river is not going to teach them to be the warriors of peace for the next generation.*

Chapter 16

ANGELA PEEKED THROUGH A gap in the closed curtain on the stage of the big auditorium in Amsterdam Rai and gaped.

"There are at least a hundred thousand people out there," she whispered to Mirembe standing in the wings, nervously shifting her weight from one foot to the other.

Tessa was behind her, prompting her speech to her once again, while her children and her husband stood a short distance away, gazing at her in admiration. It was the first time she was going to speak to such a large audience on bereavement and she was beyond nervous.

"What if I forget my speech?" she cried.

Tessa replied calmly, 'You won't; you've practiced it at least a hundred times. You know it by heart, through and through. Listen to me, Doctor Mirembe Kazosi-Okello, you've been in tougher scrapes than this. It's only saying a few words to some folks out there that will change their lives for good. Nothing more, nothing less."

"Mummy," cried Georgina, "good luck." And she blew her mother a kiss.

This helped Mirembe focus on what she was doing and why. Her daughter would stand on her shoulders and Georgina's daughter on hers, generation after generation until Africa was free and the women of her continent emerged as the proud, wise souls they truly were.

"Now get in there, Mirembe," she spoke sternly to herself, and the curtains opened wide …

LECTURING THE WORLD was tiring but invigorating, especially as most of the time she had her family with her, but Mirembe's on-going concern for Acanit's brother, Mugisha, kept her returning to Kampala as much as possible.

The young boy had been admitted to a closed unit of the psychiatric hospital, although Mirembe would have preferred to take him to Atura and treat him there. As his sister was in Kampala and he needed to be supervised by a special police force, being radicalised and still a threat to society, it made more sense to keep him in the unfamiliar hospital.

The trained psychiatrist in her had little hope when she first encountered the boy, who was angry and unhinged beyond anything she had ever encountered in her profession, but because of Acanit she wanted to do all that was in her power to save him from the bestial being he had become.

As usual her instincts proved correct. Mugisha, having not responded well to the medication and strong as an ox, managed to overpower an inattentive warden during a walk in the garden, obtained the man's gun and shot his way out. He was killed instantly by another guard. He died without having reconciled with his sister, another broken spirit of one of Africa's worst atrocities.

Mirembe cancelled all her talks and books tours to bring Acanit home to Atura to nurse her through this new loss, on which the young girl had pinned her hope for years. For a long time, she was afraid the girl's spirit was broken too, for she hovered on the brink of insanity, but the years of careful nurturing of this weak little stem proved her roots had become strong enough to weather even this storm.

"MAM, IT'S USELESS for me to think of the past only. Can you help me focus on the future? There is nothing left for me there." Acanit's weak voice sounded muffled, and listless big eyes wandered around the bedroom that had once been Mirembe's.

"Of course, darling. That's why I am here. Your future is everything to me. Listen carefully to me; from now on, this past cannot hurt you anymore. I cannot guarantee that life will not deal you other blows, but this past is gone and buried. It will not return. So much is sure." Mirembe stroked her little braids and her soft warm forehead.

"They're all dead, Mam. Do you realise? My Mummy and Daddy, Mugisha, and all my aunties and uncles and grandparents. They're all gone. I'm the only one here."

Big eyes filled with tears and Mirembe gave a sigh of relief. Tears were good, whereas this listlessness was not; tears would help her Acanit find herself again and not fall back into self-mutilation because she could not feel anything anymore.

When the girl finally slept and Mirembe slipped out of her room to make herself a cup of cocoa in the kitchen, she thought how ironical it was that she had to break off her bereavement tour because she had to help her adopted daughter's grieving. There would always be another grieving person on her path, or somewhere someone dying who needed her. A few months ago she helped Master Kevin to his final journey as well.

"Lord Universe, You have Your ways!" She wagged her finger. "It would be nice to have a break to dance and sing and be merry!"

But Mirembe immediately remembered how blessed she was with her healthy family and the little successes, such as helping Acanit and Angela find their strength.

She sat on the porch enjoying the silence of the evening and the calm thoughts in her head. What a journey it had been from a filthy, unwanted little girl to a woman inspiring people to help fellow humans in their bereavement. This was a moment to take stock and consider what the next bend in the road would herald.

Kaikara hinted at another child to complete their family, but Mirembe had so far been hesitant. She was in her late thirties now; to start all over with nappies and breast feeding? She knew what he meant, though, she felt it too; the love for a child, your own child, there was nothing like it.

It pierced your heart; it made you humble and small, yet lifted you to the top of the world and made you move mountains.

"My God, I don't understand how people survive the loss of a child," she said aloud to herself, "and what is even crazier, not to love your offspring, like my own mother."

This brought her back to thinking about Lwango and how they had discovered some form of understanding between them, but it was never an affectionate bond; there was always that feeling of alienation, mixed with Lwango's deep vexation about Mirembe's accomplishments. Her mother had not been able to keep her daughter small and ignorant as she had wanted and that gnawed at her soul. It was this that was so alien to Mirembe's outlook on life. How could you, even if you had little yourself, not wish for your child to stand on your shoulders?

"I must try to talk with her again," Mirembe said. "I want to know where that strange twist stems from."

Of course, as a doctor she understood her mother had a disorder in the Narcissistic spectrum, but both as a daughter and as a doctor she truly desired to heal her mother before her soul was beckoned to yonder side.

SHE DID NOT HAVE to wait long. When Mirembe and Kaikara returned with their children - now seven and four - to their hut on the river, Lwango showed signs of declining health.

As was her usual attitude, she ignored all ailments and kept on spreading her loud gossip and bossing around anyone near her. But her cheeks were sunken, and her eyes had lost that hard glitter that had once frightened Mirembe so much. As she promised herself, Mitrembe tried to engage in conversation with her mother every time they met, but Lwango seemed to avoid her even more than before and all she uttered had that condescending tone.

"Georgina is not as clever as Henry. I thought so. Found him reading more words than she did when I showed them the picture books with the words under the animals."

Mirembe bit her tongue not to tell her mother that she was frightening Georgina in the same way she had frightened her. She knew that would only push her mother further away, so she did what she had not since eight years old.

"Mother," she began, stressing the word 'mother' which immediately took Lwango off guard, "would you like to go with me in the car to Atura next Wednesday and have tea with me in our home there?"

Her mother eyed her suspiciously, assuming there was some sort of trick. Mirembe had never taken her there or anywhere.

"Why would I?" The old woman shrugged. "You've never cared one thing about me since you got your big madam attitude."

"I mean it, Mother. It would mean a lot to me to show you where I've grown up and to whom I owe everything I've become."

"So, you're saying you never got anything from me or your father, ungrateful child!" Her mother almost spat on the ground.

"I didn't say that. It was not my wish to be taken in by Mam and Mr Mayor."

"So, you called her Mam, did you?"

It had slipped out unnoticed. Mirembe decided to be honest with her own mother.

"Yes, she was in all ways possible my Mam, even legally so." She said it simply, expecting a torrent of words would land on her head, but it remained silent.

Having been staring at her fingernails to avoid that hard glance that still hurt her, Mirembe looked up and saw a change in her mother's eyes. The brittle, sharp look was gone and in place of it was now bewilderment and a strange sort of sorrow, almost surrender.

"What is it, Mother?" she asked. The old woman just shrugged once more. *You know, I won't give up, don't you*? the daughter said without words. *You know that at some point soon you have to meet your Maker and acknowledge how you've lived here on His earth. You're a tough cookie, Mother, but not unbreakable.*

IT WAS WONDROUS to Mirembe how she had somehow been able to get under the skin of the one woman who had never cared for her. She watched her mother sitting on her veranda with a plaid around her feet, the same plaid Mam had wrapped around Mr Mayor's legs on their first journey to Atura in the black Ford with Mam in her beige dress at the steering wheel, a shawl wrapped around her neck, and Mirembe frightened and dirty on the back seat.

Now it felt as if her mother, who had once sat daily on a similar veranda in the next street, but for decades lived in a simple hut and only bathed in the

233

river and received a new dress at Christmas, was finally back where she belonged.

Knowing that her mother had only weeks to live, Mirembe told Kaikara she would take this time out to help her mother to the other side, but that she wanted her to go in the comfort the old woman had always believed was her birthright. That was the least Mirembe could do for her.

Her mother sat leisurely, having enjoyed a long soak in a real bath and proudly wearing her new dress, her hair done by the hairdresser and her feet massaged during a pedicure.

So far that day, she had not uttered one complaint, but Mirembe was waiting for the old fox to reappear, and there it was.

"You really don't deserve all this wealth. You never lifted a finger for it."

"I know, I didn't, but I also never asked for it."

Her mother's eyes wandered towards the street and a small smile played around her lips. This was new, as Mirembe had never seen her mother smile.

"I remember seeing Oneka, your father, here in this street for the very first time. I was smitten by him from first sight."

This was actually the first time Mirembe heard her mother say anything positive about her father.

"Could you take me to his grave tomorrow?"

"Of course, Mother, we'll go after breakfast and we'll pass by the flower shop, so you can choose flowers you like."

"Your dad once bought me flowers when he had sold his fish," Lwango recalled. "I'll never forget; they were pink gardenias. But he only did that once. Think he never had enough money after that to buy me flowers."

"You'll have pink gardenias in your room every day from now on, Mother, that way you'll remember how rich you once were together with Dad."

The old woman sniffed but said nothing. Her heart was finally giving in under the weight of love from her daughter. She shifted in her chair.

"Don't fool me, girl, I know as well as you that I'm dying and that you're trying to make it up with me." She shrugged her shoulders in her particular way, but hugged the plaid closer around her legs.

"Wouldn't you want that too, Mother? Wouldn't it be better for your soul to leave in peace?"

"Probably." That came out almost too soft to be heard.

"I wouldn't want you to be out of your mind, not knowing what you're saying or doing anymore, before we have buried our hatchets, Mother. I want to do it while we're both clear-headed."

"You've got a point there, girl. I've never been one for getting soppy in old age."

"So, what is it you want to tell me? What made you set yourself so against me?" She didn't expect an answer, but wanted to ask the burning question anyway.

It was silent for a long time. They heard the church clock from the *Pentecostal Assemblies of God* chime six.

Night was approaching fast. It was getting chilly and Mirembe thought it was time to take her frail looking mother inside as she was at the end of her powers, but the old woman suddenly fired up with the old anger in her eyes.

"It was never your father, child, but he should have protected me. He should have, he should have, but he was drunk as always!"

"Mother," Mirembe cried out, alarmed by her mother's outburst, "what is the matter, what do you mean?"

Her mother calmed down somewhat and, waving her thin wrinkled arms in despair, finally broke out, "You're not Oneka's child, but the man who came to repair the boats. He took advantage of me and Oneka knew it, but he did nothing to help me for fear of getting talk in the community. That's when my anger began, and I couldn't forgive him, and I couldn't forgive you."

Mirembe clapped her hands over her mouth. Not Oneka's child, but the child of a rapist?

Was this her parents' secret, the on-going fights and her abandonment? How could it be she had never guessed anything of the sort?

"Now I understand why you called me Kabonesa, trouble being born," she said with a little voice, "but I couldn't help it, Mother, could I?"

"No, you couldn't and although I knew, I could not get over it. My mother knew too, but she also refused to help me."

"Grandma Sanyu knew?"

"Yes."

Only infrequently had Mirember seen her mother's mother in her years living in Atura, and every visit had been friendly. Never by word or deed had Sanyu given Lwango's secret away, not even the night she helped her grandmother pass over.

There were roses at Sanyu's funeral; her grandmother had loved her roses so.

MIREMBE NEEDED TIME to process this new information and, later that evening when her mother had retired to her bed, she kept pacing restlessly. She wanted to tell Kaikara - how much did he know, as his parents had been so close to hers? - but she wanted to do so face-to-face, not on the phone.

How much more she now understood her mother's grievances and her incapacity to love her and her father after what had happened.

Mirembe was finally asleep when she heard a strange noise coming from her mother's bedroom, a long, drawn out wail such as from an animal. Alarmed, she ran towards her room, slipping quickly into her dressing gown.

She found her mother lying on the floor, having thrown herself from the bed she was unfamiliar in. Again, that prolonged piercing howl sounded, which chilled her to the bone.

She squatted next to her mother and rolled her on her side, so she would be more comfortable, grabbing the blanket from the bed to cover her body, now losing its warmth. She lifted her eyelids and saw her mother was sliding quickly into a coma, but still aware.

"Mother, can you hear?" she asked, stroking the cleanly washed, white head for the first time in her life and holding the dying body against her own.

With great difficulty Lwango lifted her head and looked at her daughter. "Mirembe, forgive me," she brought out with her last strength. "You are a rising sun and I am a fallen moon. I love you, Mirembe, Mirembe, Mirembe ..."

Mumbling her daughter's name, she lost consciousness, slipping slowly from her human hands into Lord Universe's embrace.

Mirembe sat there for hours with her dying mother in her arms, feeling all the healing emotions she had always wanted to feel and never been allowed to; love, compassion, grief, forgiveness, and forever that impossible frailty of life, so precious and yet so ethereal in human hands.

THE END

Afterword

This is the short version of my speech as I created it for the *Speak to Inspire* Course and held on stage on 14 December 2018 at the London Real Headquarters. A longer version will be available for a TEDx Talk soon.

What would you do if your friend's child died?

Angela Johnson and her husband Giles are aid workers in a small village in Uganda. Through a tragic course of events they have just lost their two year old son Nathan to meningitis. Angela is sitting in the rocking chair on the veranda hugging her knees. She only realises Mirembe is there when the African lady, who lives in a hut near the river, seats herself on the steps of the porch. Angela wants to flee inside, she's not ready for visitors, almost strangers, but Mirembe doesn't speak to her. She just sits there, her hands folded in her lap, her eyes fixed on the red sun sinking below the horizon. As hours go by, Angela feels the tightness in her chest relax a little and she's grateful for the silent woman by her side.

When 4 years ago my Joy died, my beautiful 29-year old daughter destroyed by cancer, it was the single most defining moment of my life. And I had no idea how to mourn her. We have no mourning ritual like in Africa where a grieving person is not left alone. I found myself in a society where death is pushed to the fringes of our consciousness.

In one way I was fortunate, though, that my friend Mieke, who is a Chinese-trained reflexologist, insisted on giving me foot massages. Mieke strongly believes healing touch is important in the first period of bereavement and this is supported by a study published in the Journal of Clinical Nursing of 2010, which states that soothing massages after the death of a loved one can give much needed consolation and reduce stress levels.

Mourning your child is the most difficult thing a human being can do. So, it's crucial how the environment reacts to you. What I learnt in the middle of all my pain and chaos - meanwhile my second child had also been diagnosed with incurable cancer - was that what wise Euripides said is true: "Friends show love in times of trouble, not in times of happiness." I was really upset at the time by family members ignoring me and colleagues avoiding me.

Now I know they weren't being mean, they just didn't know what to say to me, unable to contemplate what it would be like to be in my shoes. I was fortunate again to have another friend, Miriam, a counselling psychologist, who said, and I quote: "It was hard to accept that I could not alleviate this suffering for you, I wanted to, but it's impossible with something so heavy and so intense. I tried not to come with empty answers as there are no answers." Both my friends were my Mirembe.

A Survey that Child Bereavement UK conducted in 2016 states that 23% of all British adults who lost a close family member wished their friends had visited them. That is one out of every four persons in this room.

Together we can bring those percentages down! We all have it in us to become a Mirembe!

I want you to think of someone you know who has been in deep mourning, even if it was years ago: be it a relative, a friend, or a colleague. Write this person a hand-written card today and tell them that you're still thinking of their loss and hope they are well. I guarantee that you'll make that person's day.

Thank you.

Hannah Ferguson
2018

32144665R00146

Printed in Poland
by Amazon Fulfillment
Poland Sp. z o.o., Wrocław